"That isn't..." Heat ripped through Lizzie when he leaned in.

"Isn't what?" Damon said. "Fair?"

"Sensible," she said as he curved a smile.

"Sensible?" he mocked, sitting back. "Is that what you are now?"

"No one stays eighteen forever, Damon."

"No," he agreed. "But, whatever age you are, you can still live and feel and dare."

"Oh, I dare," Lizzie assured him, angling her chin to stare him in the eyes. "I just don't want to be hurt again."

"Hurt?" He frowned. "Do you expect me to hurt you?"

"I just know I won't give you the chance."

"It was you who stormed off," he pointed out. She couldn't deny it. She had, Lizzie remembered. "Are you going to storm off now?" he suggested.

"As I said, I'm not eighteen."

"No. You're much improved."

The smile behind his eyes had just become dangerous. Being this close to him was dangerous enough without that hard mouth teasing her with a faint smile. Her sensible mind said, *Leave now, move away, make him take you back to the restaurant*, but it was hard to be sensible when she wanted him so much. She only had to move by the smallest degree for their lips to touch, and for Damon's arms to close around her.

And then she did, and they did, and she was lost.

Secret Heirs of Billionaires

There are some things money can't buy...

Living life at lightning pace, these magnates are no strangers to stakes at their highest. It seems they've got it all... That is until they find out that there's an unplanned item to add to their list of accomplishments!

Achieved:

1. Successful business empire

2. Beautiful women in their bed

3. *An heir to bear their name?*

Though every billionaire needs to leave his legacy in safe hands, discovering a secret heir shakes up his carefully orchestrated plan in more ways than one!

Uncover their secrets in:

Unwrapping the Castelli Secret by Caitlin Crews

Brunetti's Secret Son by Maya Blake

The Secret to Marrying Marchesi by Amanda Cinelli

Demetriou Demands His Child by Kate Hewitt

The Desert King's Secret Heir by Annie West

The Sheikh's Secret Son by Maggie Cox

The Innocent's Shameful Secret by Sara Craven

The Greek's Pleasurable Revenge by Andie Brock

Look out for more stories in the **Secret Heirs of Billionaires** series coming soon!

Susan Stephens

THE SECRET KEPT FROM THE GREEK

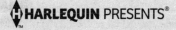
HARLEQUIN PRESENTS®

Recycling programs
for this product may
not exist in your area.

ISBN-13: 978-0-373-06081-8

The Secret Kept from the Greek

First North American Publication 2017

Copyright © 2017 by Susan Stephens

Printed in U.S.A.

Susan Stephens was a professional singer before meeting her husband on the Mediterranean island of Malta. In true Harlequin style, they met on Monday, became engaged on Friday and married three months later. Susan enjoys entertaining, travel and going to the theater. To relax she reads, cooks and plays the piano, and when she's had enough of relaxing she throws herself off mountains on skis or gallops through the countryside, singing loudly.

Books by Susan Stephens

Harlequin Presents

The Sicilian's Defiant Virgin
In the Sheikh's Service
Italian Boss, Proud Miss Prim

Wedlocked!

A Diamond for Del Rio's Housekeeper

One Night With Consequences

Bound to the Tuscan Billionaire

Hot Brazilian Nights!

In the Brazilian's Debt
At the Brazilian's Command
Brazilian's Nine Months' Notice
Back in the Brazilian's Bed

The Skavanga Diamonds

Diamond in the Desert
The Flaw in His Diamond
The Purest of Diamonds?
His Forbidden Diamond

Visit the Author Profile page at Harlequin.com for more titles.

For Kathryn...our first book together.

PROLOGUE

Eleven years previously...

LIZZIE WAS ON FIRE. He watched her brown eyes blaze bullets at him from the well of the court. She was just eighteen, with flowing red hair and—controversially at this most subdued of gatherings—black leather trousers, a skimpy top, tattoos and a pierced lip. He would have had to be unconscious not to want the force of nature that was Lizzie Montgomery

That didn't change the facts. This was a court of law, and he, Damon Gavros, was part of the team from Gavros Inc—an international shipping company registered in Greece—attending court in London. He was there to support his father, who was appearing as the chief prosecution witness in the case of Gavros Inc. versus Charles Montgomery, fraudster.

It was a shock seeing Lizzie again in court— though to say he regretted sleeping with her last night wouldn't be true. Even had he known who she was then, the fire between them would almost certainly have led them down the same road and to hell with the consequences.

They'd met for the first time the previous evening, when Lizzie, obviously distressed, had been refused a drink at the bar where he'd been sitting quietly in a corner, thinking about bringing to justice the man who had tried to defraud his father out of millions. Seeing a woman distraught, yet refusing to go home, and a barman on the point of ejecting her, he'd intervened. Taking Lizzie back to his place, he'd plied her with coffee and they'd got talking.

Lizzie was her name, she'd told him. He'd had no idea she was Charles Montgomery's daughter. She was hot, funny, and almost too happy to laugh at herself. She was looking forward to college. He was just about to leave college. One thing had led to another, and now it was too late to repair the mistake even had he wanted to.

Just how much of a mistake he was about to discover as Lizzie's father was taken down to the cells and he found Lizzie waiting for him outside the court. Her language was colourful. The slap came out of nowhere. He supposed he deserved it.

Touching his cheek, he held her blazing stare. She was half his size, but when Lizzie was roused she was a firebrand—as he had discovered last night in bed.

Uncaring of the crowd gathering around them in the expectation of a scene, she balled her fists and raged at him. 'You *bastard*! How could you have sex with me last night knowing *this* was going to happen?'

'Calm yourself, Lizzie.' He waved the Gavros legal team away. 'You're making a spectacle of yourself.'

'Calm myself?' she exclaimed bitterly. 'Thanks to you, my father's a convicted criminal!'

Charles Montgomery would always be innocent in Lizzie's eyes. As far as she was concerned the rest of the world—and most especially the man she'd clung to, panting out her lust the previous night—could go hang.

'And don't look at me like that,' she blazed. 'You don't frighten me,'

'I should hope not,' he agreed.

'Don't!' she warned, deflecting him when he reached out to comfort her.

In his peripheral vision he could see the Gavros security men politely but firmly ushering the spectators away, and now the head of his father's legal team was approaching. He waved him back too. Lizzie was due *some* consideration. Her voice was shaking with shock. The judge had wanted Lizzie's father to be an example to others who might think of following his lead, and had handed down a prison sentence lengthy enough to shock everyone in court.

'Your father hurt a lot of people, Lizzie. It wasn't just my family that suffered—'

'Stop it! *Stop it!*' she screamed, covering her ears with her hands. 'All you care about is money!'

'I have a family to protect,' he argued quietly. 'And not just my family but all those people who work for our company. Don't *they* deserve justice too?'

'And you're such a *saint*!' she yelled before swinging away.

Guilt speared him as her shoulders heaved with silent sobs. Would he have acted differently last night if he'd known this would happen? However hard he tried, he could not regret having sex with Lizzie. His only thought now was to comfort her, to shield her from curious eyes, but Lizzie Montgomery was in no mood to be consoled.

'I *hate* you!' she yelled as her friends came over to lead her away.

The words sounded torn from her soul. 'Well, I don't hate *you*,' he called after her.

Lizzie wasn't to blame for her father's actions, and however misplaced her loyalty might be he could understand it. He felt the same about *his* father, who had spent a lifetime building the business Charles Montgomery had almost destroyed.

Damon's father had always been keenly aware of the families who depended on him—a responsibility that would pass to Damon one day. He looked forward to following in the great man's footsteps. Lizzie didn't know it yet, but she was another of her father's victims. His best guess was that by the time her avaricious stepmother had finished with her Lizzie would be out on the street.

'I'd like to help you,' he offered.

'*Help* me?' Lizzie derided. 'Not this side of hell freezing over! Go back to your wealthy friends and your comfortable life, rich boy!'

Several more ripe epithets followed as Lizzie's friends tried to lead her away.

He would miss Lizzie. Who wouldn't? Even in just one night he'd seen that she was a wildcat with a heart of gold.

'My father's innocent! *Innocent!*' she yelled back at him with every ounce of strength she possessed.

'Your father's been found guilty on all counts,' he countered mildly, 'and by the highest court in this land.'

Breaking free of her friends, Lizzie spun round to face him. 'Because of you and your kind!' she raged, in a tone that was closer to an agonised howl than it was to speech. 'I'll never forgive you for this! Do you hear me? *Never!*'

He smiled faintly as he turned away. 'Never say never, Lizzie.'

CHAPTER ONE

'DAMON GAVROS! LONG TIME, no see!'

Damon Gavros! Lizzie felt weak. Surely there had to be more than one Damon Gavros in London? She could hardly breathe as Stavros, her excitable boss, burst into the busy restaurant kitchen where Lizzie was ploughing her way through a mountain of dirty dishes at the sink. No. There was no mistake. She didn't have to turn around to know it was *the* Damon Gavros when she could feel Damon in every fibre of her being. Was it really eleven years since they had last seen each other?

Steadying herself against the sink, Lizzie braced herself for an encounter she had never expected to happen—least of all here in the safety of her workplace.

Images of Damon started flashing behind her eyes. Impossibly compelling and dangerously intuitive, Damon Gavros was the only man to have made an impact on Lizzie so powerful that she had never forgotten him—never *could* forget him. And for more reasons than the fact that Damon was the most charismatic man she'd ever met.

'Welcome! Welcome!' Stavros was calling out on a steadily mounting wave of hysteria. 'Damon! *Please!* Come in to the kitchen! Follow me! I want to introduce you to everyone...'

Lizzie remained rooted to the spot. Head down, with her fists planted in the warm suds, she drew a deep, shuddering breath as a spurt of the old anger flashed through her. Standing outside that courtroom in London eleven years ago, she had never felt more alone in her life, and she had cursed Damon Gavros to hell and back for being part of the root cause of that upheaval.

Now she could see that Damon and his father had done a *good* thing, and that the fault had rested squarely with Lizzie's father, who had defrauded so many people out of their life savings. At the time she had been too confused and angry and upset to see that. It had only been when she had returned home and her stepmother had thrown her out of the house that Lizzie had finally accepted that her father was a crook and her stepmother was a heartless, greedy woman.

And Damon...?

She'd never forgotten Damon.

But where had he been for the past eleven years?

He certainly hadn't been part of Lizzie's life. Not that she held him responsible for anything except his absence. In fact she thanked him for making her life infinitely richer. She wondered what he would think of her now. She'd been such a rebel then, and now she was conventional to a fault. Would that make him suspicious?

Her body trembled with awareness as he drew closer. She hadn't felt this affected by a man in eleven long years. She'd sworn off sex after Damon—and not just because no man could compare with him.

Damon and Stavros were growing closer to the dishwashing section of the busy kitchen, and the warmth between the two men reminded Lizzie of the warmth between Damon and his father after the trial. How she'd envied them their closeness. To have someone to confide in had seemed such an impossible dream. Looking back, she could see now that the court case had done her a favour. She had learned to stand on her own feet and now, though she didn't have much, she earned her living honestly and she was free.

'Lizzie!' Stavros's voice was full of happy anticipation as he called out her name across the banks of stainless steel counters. 'May I present a very good friend of mine, recently returned from his travels...? Damon Gavros!'

She turned reluctantly.

There were a few seconds of absolute silence, and then Damon said, 'I believe we know each other.'

Damon's voice slicked through Lizzie's veins like the slide of warm cream. It was so familiar she felt as if they'd never been apart.

'That's right,' she agreed, trembling inside as she made sure to give Stavros a reassuring smile.

'I'll leave you two together,' Stavros said tactfully,

practically rubbing his hands with glee at the thought that he had finally managed to play Cupid.

'It's been a long time, Damon.'

'Indeed it has,' he agreed, scrutinising her with matching interest.

She felt vulnerable. She was hardly kitted out in her armour of choice for this reunion, in rubber overshoes, with an unflattering overall over her old clothes and an elasticated protective hat covering her wilful red curls, and her face was no doubt red and sweaty from the steam of the kitchen.

And I don't know you, she thought as she stared into a ridiculously handsome face that had only improved with age. Apart from the information in press reports about his public persona, she didn't know who Damon Gavros had become. And if he was back in London for good she had to find out.

Incredible eyes. Seductive eyes. Laughing eyes...

Dangerous eyes. They saw too much.

Damon's impact on her senses was as devastating as it had ever been—which was the only warning Lizzie needed that she should take care. From the flash of black diamonds on his crisp white cuffs to the faintly amused stare that could obliterate her sensible mind at a stroke, Damon Gavros, with his power and money, was the most terrible threat to everything Lizzie held dear.

And still her wilful body clamoured for his attention while her sensible mind screamed caution. Damon was overwhelmingly charismatic, as well as physically imposing, but it was the power of his mind that dominated everything—and that frightened her.

'Success suits you,' she said, carelessly speaking her thoughts out loud.

He gave a slight nod of acknowledgement to this, but made no reply. That was probably the best he could do, after finding her here in the kitchen.

Business pundits spoke of Damon's unparalleled success, and his monumental wealth since taking over his father's company. When their articles weren't referring to him as the world's most eligible bachelor, they were dubbing him the benevolent billionaire, because of his charitable interests. She doubted he'd feel charitably disposed towards *her* if he discovered how she'd lived for the past eleven years.

Tamping down her alarm, Lizzie accepted that they'd both changed. She was more savvy, and better able to handle Damon.

'Why don't we get out of here?' he suggested.

'I beg your pardon?' She looked at him in surprise, thinking she must have misheard him.

'I'm not keen on holding our reunion here, are you?'

His stare seared through her, and for a moment she didn't know what to say. The thought of going anywhere with Damon Gavros was alarming.

Damon could understand Lizzie's surprise at seeing him. Seeing her had been a shock for him too—especially finding her so changed. He was keen to know what had been happening to Lizzie over the past eleven years, and why on earth she was working here.

'I'm sure Stavros can spare you for an hour or so,' he insisted.

Confident that Lizzie would follow him, he was already halfway to the door.

'I can't,' she said flatly, bringing him to a halt. 'As you can see…' She spread her hands wide in the ugly rubber gloves when he turned around. 'I'm working.'

It had never occurred to him that she might say no. 'Stavros?' he queried, turning his attention to her boss, who was hovering at the back of the kitchen.

'Of course,' Stavros insisted with enthusiasm. 'Lizzie deserves a break. She can join you at your table. My chefs will prepare a feast—'

'I'd rather not,' Lizzie interrupted.

Damon had caught a glimpse of shabby jeans and a faded top beneath Lizzie's overall and could understand her reservations. Stavros's restaurant was seriously high-end, but now they'd met again he was determined to find out everything about her, and bury the hatchet so many years after her father's trial.

'We don't have to eat here—somewhere casual?' he suggested. 'Another time, Stavros,' he was quick to add, with a reassuring smile for his hovering host. 'I'd like the chance to fill in the past eleven years, wouldn't you?' he said, turning to Lizzie.

She gave a nervous laugh. This was so unlike the Lizzie he'd known that he felt instantly suspicious. 'Unless your eleven years includes a husband or a fiancé?'

'No,' she said, lifting her chin to regard him steadily. 'It doesn't.'

'Then, do you have a coat?'

'Yes, but—'

'An hour or so of your time?' He shrugged. 'What harm can that do?'

Stavros intervened before she could reply. 'How can you refuse?' Stavros asked Lizzie, with a warm smile and an expansive gesture so typical of the genial restaurateur. 'I'll get someone to take over your work. Go now,' he chivvied, 'Lizzie never takes time off,' he confided to Damon. 'Half an hour for old times' sake?' he urged Lizzie, doing Damon's work for him.

Short of being rude to both of them, there was only one thing Lizzie could do.

'I'll get my coat,' she said.

She went to the staff bathroom and sluiced her face in cold water. Staring at herself in the mirror above the sink, she wondered where eleven years had gone. Did it matter? Damon Gavros was back. She had to handle it.

At least Stavros was delighted. He was always trying to fix her up with a man. *Billionaire and potwasher?* Even Stavros couldn't make *that* one fly, though Damon seemed happy enough. That had better not have been a smile of *triumph* on his lips. Lips that had kissed her into oblivion, Lizzie remembered, trying not to think back to the most significant night of her life.

Her heart jumped when she walked out of the re-
restroom to find Damon relaxed back against the wall.
Had he always been so hot?

Yes, she thought, smiling politely as he insisted
on helping her with her coat.

To his credit, his expression didn't falter, though
her coat, with its plucked threads and plastic buttons,
and a collar that had already been bald when she'd
bought it in the thrift shop, was miles too big for her.
She'd just needed something warm, while Damon's
coat had probably been custom-made. It was a soft
alpaca overcoat, in a blue so dark it was almost black.

With a cashmere scarf slung casually around his
neck, he looked like the master of the sexual universe.
He had to be thinking, *What the hell has happened
to Lizzie Montgomery?*

Life. Life had happened to Lizzie Montgomery,
Lizzie reflected as Damon held the door. And life
changed people. For the better, she could only hope,
in both their cases.

'I'm driving myself tonight,' Damon explained
as he stopped by the passenger door of a fabulous
brand-new black Bentley with a personalised number plate: DG1.

'Of course you are,' she teased in a pale imitation
of her old self. 'Chauffeur's night off?' she suggested.

Damon chose not to answer as he opened the passenger door. The scent of money and leather assailed
her the moment she sank into, rather than perched
on, the most incredibly comfortable pale cream kid-
skin seat.

'This is lovely,' she observed, looking around as Damon slid in beside her.

She didn't want him to think she was so downtrodden and disadvantaged that she was overwhelmed by his obvious wealth. She'd been bold when they'd first met, and now, in spite of how she must appear to Damon, she had everything she could possibly need. He might have made millions, and she might be poor, but there were more ways than one to feel a deep sense of satisfaction with life and she'd got that.

When Damon started the engine it purred—in contrast to the jangling conflict inside Lizzie. Pulling smoothly away from the kerb, he joined the sluggish London evening traffic. This was how the rich travelled, she concluded. They didn't bounce along, crushed on every side in an over-full rush hour bus. They glided in their opulent private space, enjoying classical music playing softly in the background.

'Do you enjoy your job?'

The blunt question jolted Lizzie back to the unlikely reality of being cocooned inside the most luxurious vehicle in London with the world's most eligible bachelor.

'Yes,' she confirmed, lifting her chin. 'I have great friends at the restaurant—especially Stavros. I'm exactly where I want to be, working alongside genuine people who care for me as I care for them.'

Damon seemed taken aback for a moment, and then he said, 'Hungry?'

She was—and for more than food, she realised as Damon flashed a glance her way. She hadn't felt like this in eleven years, but he only had to look at her for her to remember how it had felt to be in his arms. Which was a complete waste of good thinking time, she accepted, drawing her shabby coat closer around her trembling body.

'Surprising even myself, I'm hungry too,' he admitted.

'You can take me back.'

'Now, why would I do that?'

She stared down in shock as his hand covered hers. He'd better not be feeling sorry for her.

He drew the Bentley to a halt on the Embankment running alongside the river Thames. By the time she had released her seat belt he was opening her door. It was such a romantic view it took her attention for a moment.

'Burger or hot dog?' he said.

She almost laughed. Perhaps it was just as well he'd shaken her away from the romantic sight of the Palace of Westminster and stately Big Ben. It wouldn't do to lose focus around Damon. 'Hot dog, please.'

'Ketchup and mustard?'

'Why not be lavish?' she said.

He gave her a look and turned away, allowing her to take in the powerful spread of his shoulders as he started chatting easily to the guy behind the food stand not far from where they had parked. Damon had always got on well with everyone—but how would he handle what she had to tell him?

Not yet, she decided. She would have to know this

older, shrewder Damon better before she could tell him everything. She had to know what made him tick and how he lived his life.

As he handed the hot dog over their fingers touched and a quiver of awareness ran through her. It seemed that however hard she tried to remain detached, so she could think straight, her body insisted on going its own way. And her body wanted Damon as much as it ever had.

'Thinking back?' he said, reading her mind.

Thinking back to when she had been an eighteen-year-old virgin with nothing certain in her future except that it would change? Yes—unfortunately. 'I'm thinking maybe I have too much sauce?' she suggested.

'You *always* had too much sauce,' Damon observed.

She decided to ignore the jibe. Damon was standing under a street lamp, leaning back against it, and the spotlight suited him. He was so dark and swarthy—so compelling in every way. The shadowed light only enhanced his sculpted features.

'I didn't realise how hungry I was,' she said, biting down hard on the delicious snack in an attempt to distract herself from Damon's brazen physicality. And, truthfully, it was a treat to have someone other than Stavros buy her a meal and to care a damn if she enjoyed it.

'Where did you disappear to after the trial?' he asked with a frown.

'Where did I "disappear to"?' she repeated thoughtfully.

Good question. Not to a loving home—that was for sure.

'Who'll support me now?' That had been Lizzie's stepmother's first question when Lizzie had returned home to find her suitcases waiting in the hall.

She should have known what was happening, but she had rushed up to her bedroom, thinking to bury her grief in her pillows, only to find her bedroom had been cleared. She had wasted a few precious minutes railing against fate before pulling herself together and accepting that this was her life now, and she'd better get on with it.

On her way out of the house she'd found her stepmother in her father's study, going through the drawers of his desk. 'I guess we'll both have to work,' Lizzie had said.

Her stepmother's expression had twisted into something ugly. 'I don't *work*,' she'd said haughtily. 'And if you think you can persuade me to let you stay, you're wasting your time. You're one expense I can't afford.'

That had been the last time they'd seen each other, and it had taken Lizzie's stepmother less than a week to replace Lizzie's father with a richer man.

She decided on a heavily edited version for Damon. 'It wasn't all bad,' she said, thinking back. 'The shock of finding myself homeless was good for me. I had to stand on my own two feet, and I found I enjoyed doing it.'

'Sacrificing your dreams?' He frowned.

'Sometimes dreams have to wait,' Lizzie said

frankly. She'd done more than survive. She'd thrived, and had proved herself capable of far more than she'd imagined.

'You've got ketchup on your chin—'

She sucked in a fast breath as he wiped it off. His touch was still electric.

'Next time I'll take you out for a proper meal—'

'Next time?' she queried. 'So you're back for good?' Her heart drummed a tattoo as she thought about all the implications of that.

He chose not to answer her question. 'Stavros says you work too hard. You have to take a break some-time,' he insisted.

What else had Stavros told him? she wondered. She had so much to lose. Damon had been absent from her life for a long time, but he was still a core part of her existence. He didn't know it yet, but he could rip her world apart on a whim.

'Soda or water?' he asked.

'Water, please.' Her throat was tight and dry.

As Damon turned to speak to the vendor she thought back to her first deception on their night to-gether, when she'd been a virgin pretending not to be, embarking on a romantic adventure with a hand-some Greek—or so she'd thought. Her life had been in chaos at the time. She hadn't been thinking straight. Hated by her stepmother, she'd been desperate for her father to notice her.

She'd failed.

She'd almost failed with Damon too. Clinging to him, begging him to take her so she could forget her wretched home life, she had exclaimed with shock as he'd taken her, and he'd pulled back. It had taken all her feminine wiles to persuade him to continue.

Of course she was on the pill, she'd insisted.

He'd used protection anyway.

Belt and braces? she'd teased him.

Damon had proved to be a master of seduction, a master of pleasure, and they'd made love all night. But there had been chances to talk too, and it had been then that they had discovered a closeness that neither of them had expected. Surprising both of them, she was sure, they had enjoyed each other's company.

'Let's walk.'

She glanced up as Damon took the top off her bottle of water. 'I'd like that.'

A walk promised a welcome break from the past. She could take in the majesty of London instead... that was if she could stop looking at Damon.

Life and responsibility had cut harsh lines into his brow and around his mouth, but those only made him seem more human. Harsh, yet humorous, ruthless, yet empathetic, Damon was an exceptional man.

'When I'm in London I walk a lot,' he revealed, glancing down, his eyes too dark to read. 'Sometimes it's good to be alone with your thoughts, don't you think?'

'That depends who you are and what you're thinking, I suppose,' she said, remembering how quickly their whispered confidences in bed had turned to mistrust the following day in court. It would take more than walking together to clear the air between them, she suspected.

At the time the press reports—coming on top of everything else that had been happening at home—had destroyed Lizzie's confidence. She'd lost her self-belief, as well as her confidence in her own judgement. She'd lost her trust in everyone—and in herself most of all. But then she'd realised that with no one to pick her up she'd better get on with it, and so she'd rebuilt her life along very different lines, far away from privilege and trickery.

A pawnbroker had given Lizzie her first break, taking what few scraps had remained of her mother's jewellery in exchange for enough money to pay her first week's rent. She remembered begging him not to sell her mother's wedding ring. 'There's nothing exceptional about it,' she'd protested when he'd informed her that he wasn't a charitable institution. 'You must have dozens like it—'

'Not with three seed pearls set in the centre of the band,' he'd said as he'd studied the ring with his eyeglass.

'I'll clean your shop for nothing,' she'd offered in desperation. 'I'll pay you back with interest, I promise...'

But life had caught up with her, making the necessity of keeping a roof over her head more important than her mother's wedding ring, so it would have to wait. Maybe one day...

'Something wrong?' Damon asked as she bit her lip and grimaced.

'Nothing. Why?' she gazed up at him evenly.

'You made a sound like an angry kitten.'

She made no comment. Being compared to a kitten would not have been her choice. She felt as if the past few years had required her to be a tigress.

'Enough?' he said, when she shivered.

'I'd better get back,' she agreed.

The Bentley sat waiting for them, gleaming black and opulent. It was attracting admiring glances from passers-by, and now they were attracting interest too, as they approached it. The elegant vehicle was a fabulous representation of privilege, and Lizzie thought it the most visible proof of the yawning gulf between them. She couldn't imagine what people must be thinking about the suave billionaire and the shabby kitchen worker getting into a car like that.

Did there ever come a point when a cork stopped bobbing to the surface? she wondered as Damon opened the passenger door and saw her safely settled in?

No. She hadn't come this far to give up now.

'Home?' he asked.

So he could see where she lived?

'Back to the restaurant, please.' She tried not to look at him. 'There are things I need to pick up.'

She didn't want him visiting her home. She couldn't risk it. This had been pleasant, but there was more to life than Damon's riches and his personal success. What Lizzie was protecting was infinitely more precious, and she had no intention of risking everything she cared about by acting carelessly now.

Damon had the power to steal everything away from her.

She wouldn't let him. It was as simple as that. Whatever it took, that wasn't going to happen.

He started the engine and the Bentley purred obediently.

'Your mother was Greek, wasn't she?' he asked conversationally as he pulled onto the road.

'Yes, she was.'

'I suppose that accounts for your unusual colouring. I never thought about it before, but with your Celtic red hair and those chocolate-brown eyes and long black lashes your colouring is quite unusual...'

'I suppose it is,' Lizzie agreed, realising that she had never thought about it either, beyond the fact that when things had been at their bleakest she had sought refuge in the warm, home-loving Greek community in London, where there was always someone who knew someone, she reflected wryly. But wasn't life like that? Paths crossed, then separated, and then crossed again.

'I think we should see each other again.'

She stared at Damon in amazement, feeling a little defensive. 'Should we? Why?' Her heart thundered as she waited for his reply.

He shrugged. 'I promised you a proper meal?'

'I won't hold you to that.' But they would *have* to see each other again, she accepted. That was inevitable now.

'We'll make a date before I leave tonight,' he said, glancing across at her.

Would they? Could she risk spending an entire evening with Damon? Could she risk becoming relaxed with him and yet not telling him about anything of significance that had happened in her life over the past eleven years? Could she risk her feelings for him only to lose him again—and for good this time?

She had never shrunk from a challenge yet, Lizzie concluded as Damon slowed the Bentley outside the restaurant, whether that challenge had been battling the demand for clean plates when Stavros's industrial-sized dishwashers decided to pack up in the middle of service—or having a second meeting with the man who didn't know he was the father of her ten-year-old child.

CHAPTER TWO

No ONE—NOT even the tall, imposing figure towering over her as he opened the car door and stood back—would ever come between Lizzie and her daughter.

Thea had never asked about her father. In fact Thea had shrugged off all mention of a father, which Lizzie had come to think was for the best when it had proved impossible to get in touch with Damon.

Lizzie's experience with her *own* father was hardly encouraging. She had never got past the fact that he'd rejected her. Lizzie's mother had been an heiress, and had had an obvious use, but once her mother was dead and the money was spent Lizzie's father had lost interest in her.

Lizzie had been too young to understand at the time, but she still remembered her wonderful mother being sad and wanting Lizzie to have a better and more exciting life. Maybe that had fuelled Lizzie's night of rebellion with Damon. It was very easy to mistake lust for love at eighteen—as it was to take a late, loving parent's suggestion and bend it to suit her own, hormonal eighteen-year-old's will.

'Goodnight, Damon, and thank you—'

'Not so fast,' he said, catching hold of her arm. 'We haven't made that date yet.'

'Do you really want to?'

'Do you need to consult your diary?' he countered.

'I do have other things to do,' she pointed out.

'But nothing important, I'm sure…?'

Damon's black stare bored into her. She had to think of something fast—and that something didn't include blurting out that they had a child together, here on a busy London street.

'Why don't you come back to the restaurant some time?' *And give me time to think and plan how best to tell Thea about this.* 'I'm usually there each night, and we can fix something up.'

'No kidding?' he murmured.

Letting her go, he pulled back.

She watched Damon drive away in his Bentley until the limousine had turned the corner and was out of sight. The logic she'd used at eighteen for keeping her pregnancy to herself felt more like a selfish cop-out now. Yes, she'd been facing huge upheaval in her life—and, yes, it had been a fight to survive, with her character largely unformed and her reaction to crises untested—but maybe she could have done something differently, or better.

But when Thea had been born Lizzie had wanted to protect her from the hurt Lizzie had felt when *her* father had rejected her. She didn't know that it wouldn't happen to Thea. Why would Damon want a child?

As the years had passed and her conscience had pricked she'd tried to get in touch with him, but his people had kept her away. And then, in another unexpected turn, Thea had proved to be musically gifted—a talent Lizzie believed Thea had inherited from *her* mother. Lizzie's mother had used to say she had music flowing through her veins instead of blood. And once Thea's musical life had taken off, Lizzie had been completely wrapped up in that. Thea had recently won a music scholarship to a prestigious school in London, where she was a boarder.

Didn't Damon deserve to know all this?

'Back already?' Stavros exclaimed with obvious disappointment. 'You don't look happy, Lizzie-*itsa*. What's wrong?'

'I had a lovely time,' she insisted, determined to wipe the concern from Stavros's face. 'And I've come back to help you to clear up for the night.'

'You shouldn't have come back. You deserve a little happiness,' Stavros complained with a theatrical gesture.

Did she? She was guilty of failing to contact Damon, because keeping him in the dark had allowed Lizzie to carry on her life with Thea without the interference of a very powerful and wealthy man. She would be lying if she said she didn't feel threatened now.

She would have to tell him about Thea, Lizzie realised as she set to and got to work, but she would choose the time.

Which would mean seeing him again!

Anxiety washed over her in hot and cold waves. There was a more important thing to do first—and that was to prepare Thea for the fact that her father was back.

Lizzie Montgomery! He couldn't believe he'd found her again.

Was it a coincidence?

Opening the front door to his penthouse apartment, located on the top floor of one of the most iconic landmarks in London, he accepted that he'd just visited one of the most popular Greek restaurants in London, and with the way the grapevine worked, someone had always been bound to know Lizzie.

Coincidence or not, being close to the woman he hadn't been able to get out of his mind for more than ten years had been the most extraordinary experience. Seeing Lizzie again had reminded him of a night that hadn't been just about sex—though the sex had been more than memorable.

Pouring a Scotch, he strolled to the window and stared out across the London skyline. The shallow society beauties he normally wheeled out for public events bored him. Where sex was concerned, they couldn't keep up. He was a hard, driven, solitary man, whose life revolved around his work.

And he hadn't been back in London five minutes before the first thing he did was to search out all things Greek.

Maybe to find Lizzie?

Okay, so he had. What of it?

He remembered Lizzie mentioning her love of her mother's country, its culture and its cuisine, that night. She'd love to visit Greece one day, she'd told him when they had been lying side by side in bed, sated, with their limbs entwined.

He *would* see her again. It was inevitable. Eleven years couldn't simply be dismissed over a hot dog with ketchup and mustard. Especially when his intuition told him that Lizzie was holding back more than she was telling him. He wanted to know why she was washing pots when she'd had such big dreams. What was holding her back?

He'd succeeded by working as his father had—alongside men and women who were his friends. Granted, he'd had every advantage. His father was a good man, while Lizzie's father had been a swindler and a cheat who had sucked his victims dry, but that still didn't explain why Lizzie was working in a restaurant, washing dishes.

Would she thank him for interfering in her life?

Did he care?

He took a deep swallow of Scotch and tried to imagine her life after the trial. However she'd played it, it couldn't have been easy for her when he'd walked into Stavros's kitchen to find her at the sink. He *would* buy her that meal. He owed her that much, and he wanted to know more about her.

'Can I get you a drink, sir?' the waiter behind the bar at Stavros's restaurant asked him the next evening, when he returned to the restaurant.

'I'm not staying,' he explained. 'Could you please tell Ms Montgomery that there's somebody waiting to see her at the bar?'

'Of course, sir.'

As the waiter hurried away he cast his mind back to that other night. He couldn't remember talking to anyone as he'd talked to Lizzie that night. She'd trusted him, he remembered with a stab of guilt. He had never expected to find the happiness his parents had enjoyed for forty years, but that night he'd thought he could find some temporary distraction with Lizzie—until the shock of discovering who she was at the trial.

No one had ever stood up to him as she had. He admired her for that.

He glanced towards the kitchen, wondering what was keeping her. His body tightened on the thought that she was only yards away. Pushing back from the bar, he stood up. He couldn't wait any longer for her to come to him.

'No.' Lizzie held up her hand as soon as she caught sight of him. 'You can't just walk in. You've got to warn me first.'

'With a fanfare?' he suggested with a look.

'You can't walk into my place of work, looking like a…a Hell's Angel,' she exclaimed with frustration as her glance roved slowly over him, 'and demand that I leave with you right away.'

He lips pressed down and he shrugged. 'You won't need your overall.'

She huffed and gazed skywards. 'Thanks for the charming invitation—but, no.'

Undaunted, he pressed on dryly. 'It's a great night for a bike ride.'

'Then go and enjoy it,' she suggested.

'You don't mean that.'

She raised a brow.

'If Lizzie wants time off she can have it,' Stavros announced, appearing like a genie out of a bottle from the pantry. 'No one works harder than Lizzie-*itsa*. I keep telling her she should get out more—treat herself to some new clothes, and a hairdo while she's at it—'

'There's nothing wrong with Lizzie,' he said, maintaining eye contact with her.

'Of course not,' Stavros placated. 'It's just that she puts everyone else first.'

'As do you, my old friend,' he said, feeling guilty that he'd shut Stavros out. 'Shall we go?' he added to Lizzie, who was still staring at him mutinously.

She had never looked more beautiful. Her shapeless apron and clumpy overshoes tried to strip away her femininity but failed utterly in his eyes. Even with those bright red curls, made frizzy by the heat in the kitchen, peeping out from under the ugly cap, she was beautiful.

The loose ends from eleven years ago had never been in more need of tying up.

'So you couldn't stay away?' she challenged.

The way she stared him directly in the eyes made his senses roar. 'That's right,' he agreed.

'You're *do* know you're in the way? This is a busy professional kitchen—'

'Then leave with me and the congestion will clear.' He angled his chin to smile into her eyes.

'You're impossible!' she complained.

'I'll see you outside,' he told her.

'In your dreams,' she flashed.

He had *great* dreams.

He caught a glimpse of Lizzie's eyes darkening as he left the kitchen. If she only knew how he wanted to drag her away from that sink and lower her, naked, into a warm, foaming bath, where he would wash her, pleasure her and make love to her until she couldn't stand up, she might not be reaching for her coat now.

How had he stayed away for eleven years? Yes, he'd been working tirelessly to rebuild the damage done to his father's business, so his parents could re-tire in comfort, but he'd taken himself away to the furthest reaches of the world in an attempt to lose himself to everything familiar. And there, in the seemingly endless miles of the desert, he had found himself, and a purpose, which was to help those who had not been as lucky as he had. Why had he needed to get away, and to do this? Was it penance for the shame felt at the way he'd treated Lizzie—the way he'd turned his back on her after the trial?

'Don't keep me waiting,' he warned her. He was eager to pick up the threads he'd left loose for the past eleven years and weave them into a pattern he could understand.

* * *

Damon was waiting for her outside on a bike. Whatever next? It was a monster of a thing—big and black, purring rhythmically beneath him. In the deep dark shadows of the night, sitting astride the throbbing motorbike, Damon Gavros was quite simply the hottest thing on two hard-muscled legs.

He handed her a helmet and helped her put it on. She tried not to react when his fingertips brushed her skin, sending tidal waves of sensation streaking through her.

'Just a short ride,' she warned—a warning for herself more than him. 'Is there an approved way of mounting this thing?'

Damon laughed as he secured his helmet, lowering the black visor so she could no longer see his eyes. 'You have to climb on behind me and put your arms around my waist.'

There was every reason not to do so.

'You'll have to relax,' he said when she tried to keep her distance. 'And hold on.'

She might have yelped when the bike surged forward. She wasn't sure. She was too distracted by Damon…by *holding* Damon. The power of the bike throbbing between her legs didn't help.

Damon judged the traffic expertly, and soon they were moving smoothly through the night. Of all places, he took her to a funfair. She supposed it was neutral ground, where there wasn't much option but to relax. There was certainly plenty of noise and colour, and dazzling flashing lights.

Dismounting from the bike, she removed the helmet, then glanced at Damon's outstretched hand. 'Maybe this isn't such a good idea,' she said, pulling back.

'This is an *excellent* idea,' he insisted.

She remembered, then, that Damon's easy charm was as much a part of his nature as the steely side that had played its part in condemning her father to a lifetime in jail—a punishment that had almost certainly led to his early death.

Maybe it seemed odd that she was mourning her father's passing, but however he had treated Lizzie she still thought him weak rather than bad. He certainly hadn't stood a chance against the Gavros team.

'Lizzie?'

Damon's voice brought her plummeting back from an uncomfortable past to an incredible present.

And the future...?

She preferred not to think about that. Not yet. She would. Of course she would. But not while Damon's shrewd eyes were searching hers. She would choose the time, and she would choose the place, and it wasn't now.

He bought tickets for the big wheel. As she climbed into the small cabin and the door closed on the two of them, trapping Lizzie inside with her memories and with Damon, it was hardly reassuring to discover that her body instantly responded to his heat and his strength, reminding her with painful attention to detail of how it had felt to be naked in his arms.

'You've turned pale. It's not too high for you, is it?'

'I'm certainly out of my comfort zone,' she admitted, thinking about Thea, and how Damon was likely to respond when he found out they had a daughter together. 'It's a long way down…' she mused quietly.

'You look exhausted,' he observed.

'It's hard work in a professional kitchen, and I've got more than one job.' He could easily find that out. Better she tell him than that he started sleuthing. She needed the money to pay the rent, and to cover all the extras at Thea's school.

'Don't you ever take time off?' he pressed.

'Hardly ever,' she admitted. And what time she had, she spent with Thea.

'And you live alone?'

The big wheel was a mistake. She couldn't get away from Damon's questions. To answer him meant telling him that she lived on her own most of the time—even in the school holidays—and Thea was often away, playing with the orchestra. Lizzie tried to go with her when she could, which meant finding a job in a bar, or as waiting staff to pay her way.

Their next trip was to Greece.

'Lizzie?'

'Yes. I live alone,' she said, quickly pulling herself together.

'It must have been a long road back for you?'

It was hard to concentrate. All she could think about now was Thea's upcoming trip to Greece.

"Lizzie?' I said it must have been a long road back for you?'

'I like my work,' she said distractedly.

'But it's repetitive,' Damon pointed out, 'and with no personal reward—'

'Apart from earning my living and keeping my pride intact, do you mean?'

'I didn't mean to offend you. I'm just curious.'

And now she was all heated up. How dared Damon stride back into her life and start judging her?

Wouldn't Thea be happier with a father who could give her so much more than she could?

No. She would not, Lizzie thought fiercely. 'Let's get one thing straight,' she said on the wave of that thought. 'I don't need your pity.'

'And you won't get it,' Damon assured her with matching force.

CHAPTER THREE

BUT IT WASN'T long before Damon was questioning her again. 'So what happened to your dream of attending that art college in Switzerland?' he pressed as their cabin sank steadily towards the ground

'I had lots of dreams when I was eighteen.'

Unfortunately they hadn't tallied with her step-mother's plans for Lizzie, and as those dreams would have been paid for by her father, using other people's money—mostly Damon's family's—Lizzie realised now they had been meaningless.

'I owe you an apology.'

'For showing loyalty to your father?'

Damon read her so easily, Lizzie thought as his powerful shoulders lifted in a shrug.

'You don't owe me a thing,' he insisted.

Their stares met and held for a potent few seconds, but all that did was allow Lizzie time to consider the big truth she wasn't telling Damon. She couldn't tell him yet. Not until she was sure of him—or as sure as she could be.

'We were discussing your dreams?' he prompted.

'*You* were,' she argued, with a spark of her old dry humour. 'Life's a series of compromises, don't you think? If you can't adjust, you flounder.'

'And you've had to do a lot of adjusting?' Damon guessed.

She remained silent.

'I can't imagine you floundering,' he admitted. 'Even at eighteen you had a good head on your—'

'Reckless shoulders?' Lizzie supplied. 'I had too much emotion in play back then.'

'And not enough now?'

His suggestion silenced her. Damon's searching glance was disturbing in all sorts of ways. She couldn't regret her rebellion eleven years ago, or her search for one night of love—which was probably the best way to describe the most memorable night of her life. How could she regret anything, when making love with Damon had created Thea?

'Penny for them?'

The smile that could heat her from the inside out was back, tugging at the corner of his mouth. 'You wouldn't want to know.'

'Try me,' he pressed.

Confide her concerns in him? Tell him how much of a struggle it was to keep the boat afloat, or that when Thea needed something for school Lizzie couldn't always guarantee she'd come through? This was the man who had walked out of her life without a backward glance—as her father had. This was the man she had been unable to reach again and again. She had to remember that—always. She couldn't face that coldness again. She had more pride than to do so. And more love for Thea than to allow her precious daughter to live through something similar.

And there was another way of looking at it. Damon might not *want* to know. What respectable billionaire would want to hear that he had a child with the daughter of a convicted felon? Would Damon believe Thea *was* his child? The shame of her father's crime had tainted Lizzie. Sometimes she believed she would never throw it off. That same shame taunted her now, with the thought that even if Damon were prepared to accept that Thea was his daughter he might not entrust her to Lizzie's care?

Whatever the consequences, her course was clear. She must first tell Thea, and then Damon.

'We're down,' he said, startling her.

'Yes…right…' she said, glancing around to see the cabin had settled on its stand. 'What a relief.'

'Vertigo can be devastating, can't it?' Damon commented, but his look was shrewd and it stripped her lie bare.

They didn't stay at the funfair. By mutual silent consent, they headed back to the bike.

'Where did you live when you left home after the court case?' Damon asked as the noise of the fair began to fade into the background.

'On a park bench,' Lizzie said bluntly, thinking back.

'I'm being serious,' Damon insisted.

'And so am I,' she admitted. 'I spent the first night

on a park bench—well, most of it…until it started raining.'

'And then?' His face had tightened into a grim mask.

Lizzie thought back to her first and thankfully her only terrifying, freezing night as a homeless person. She had quickly figured out that she must find a place to live fast or, quite simply, her appearance and the fact that she couldn't wash properly would make respectable people turn her away. With no money, that had meant finding a job—*any* job.

'I got a job the next morning,' she remembered. 'As a cleaner. I was good at that. I'd had plenty of experience,' she said dryly. 'My stepmother was too mean to pay anyone to do her cleaning, but she had me and she was very particular. It stood me in good stead,' she admitted.

'I can imagine.'

Could he imagine the woman who had insisted Lizzie must clean the floors on her hands and knees, rather than with a mop, and take a toothbrush to the corners of the room? Could he imagine that same woman making Lizzie do it all over again, after her stepmother had thoughtlessly trampled on the floor in her muddy boots?

'Actually, the cleaning jobs I managed to get were easy after my work at home,' she reflected.

'And where do you live now?'

'Haven't you asked Stavros?'

Damon dipped his chin to stare into her eyes. 'That's not fair.'

'You're right,' she agreed as they drew to a halt in front of the bike. 'Stavros has been nothing but kind to me.'

'Whereas I haven't?'

'You've only just come back to London. It remains to be seen,' she said bluntly.

'What makes you think I'd want to investigate your life?'

'Nothing,' she said quickly—too quickly. 'I have a small bedsit, if you're interested.'

'I *am*,' Damon insisted as he picked up her helmet.

'I know that look,' she said.

He frowned. 'What look?'

'The look that says, *She grew up like a princess and her fall has been swift and hard*. I can't tell you how many times I've seen that same look over the years. But you should know that I've never been happier than I am now.'

That was the truth, Lizzie reflected, calming down. She had a daughter who loved her, and jobs that paid the rent. And, yes, it was tough sometimes, but she had never once fallen into debt.

'Okay?' she challenged Damon as he handed over her helmet. 'Are we done with the third degree now?'

'We're done,' he conceded.

'I think we should talk about *you* for a change—'

'No,' he said flatly, startling her into silence with the force of his response. 'I'm a very private man.'

'Then perhaps you should understand how I feel.'

Damon regarded her coolly. 'Aren't you going to get on the bike?'

'Shall I salute first?'

He gave her a look that might make some people blink, but it only made Lizzie more determined to stand up to him.

This had definitely been an interesting encounter, Lizzie concluded as they roared back to the city. Neither of them was exactly soft or malleable. She had a daughter to protect, which gave her mama tiger claws as well as an iron will, while Damon was the hardest man she knew by some margin. For all his outward charm, which he could turn on when it suited him, Damon Gavros was rock through and through.

He drew to a halt outside the restaurant. 'Drink?' he suggested as she removed her helmet.

'I don't think so, but thank you—it's been an interesting evening.'

'One drink,' he insisted, getting off the bike.

In spite of her reservations, she had to admit that it was a pleasant change to be *this* side of the tastefully lit bar. Stavros had peeped around the kitchen door and had then retired with a broad smile on his face. That in itself was worth the sacrifice of sitting with Damon. All the drinks were on the house, the barman insisted, but Damon still paid.

'So,' he said, glancing at her over his bottle of beer. 'Tell me more about your stepmother, Cinderella.'

'Less of that,' she warned. 'There's nothing needy about *me*.'

Damon's lips pressed down, almost as if he agreed. 'So…she sounds like a fascinating character?' he pressed.

'Luminous,' Lizzie said dryly.

She would credit her stepmother with one thing: she'd helped Lizzie to face reality fast. Before her stepmother had arrived on the scene Lizzie would have been the first to admit she'd been spoiled. She might have reached adulthood with no concept of responsibility if she hadn't been thrown out of the house, had her faith in her father destroyed, her dreams crushed, *and* discovered she was pregnant— all in one and the same month. That would have been enough to wake the dead. And she certainly wasn't spoiled now. Her life was devoted to Thea.

'I don't want to talk about me. It's your turn,' she said.

'Maybe it's time for me to go,' Damon countered.

'Please yourself.' Burying her face in her glass of water, she sucked on the straw, refusing to say any more about a time when life had seemed to stretch ahead of her in an endless stream of promise—promise that had turned out to be fantasy.

Her father had appeared to have money to burn when she was young. Now she knew it had been other people's money he was burning—Gavros money, mostly. Nothing made him happier than lavishing money on his darling daughter, her father had told her as they'd planned one treat after another.

He'd been showing off to her stepmother, she realised now; hoping to catch another big fish like Lizzie's mother, the heiress. The joke of it was, the woman he'd chosen to bring home as his second wife had been a chancer like him, captivated by his apparent wealth.

Thinking her father was lonely, Lizzie had welcomed her stepmother to begin with. She had wanted nothing more than to see her father happy again. It hadn't taken long to find out how wrong she could be.

'You told me that night that you loved to paint,' Damon reminded her. 'Another dream down?' he suggested.

'I don't have time to dream now.'

'That sounds dull.'

So dull he stood up to go.

'I'll take you home,' he offered.

'No need,' Lizzie insisted quickly. 'Stavros arranges a cab for staff when we stay late.'

Damon nodded his head. 'Okay. Another time.'

Or maybe not. She wasn't sure she could live through this tension again. Wanting someone and knowing they were out of reach for ever was a torture she could well do without.

'You must enjoy heading up the family business,' she observed, for the sake of maintaining polite chit-chat as she walked him to the door. 'The press refers to you as a billionaire—'

'I hope I'm more than that.'

She could have cut off her tongue. The way Damon was staring at her made her wonder if he thought she was a mercenary chip off her father's swindling old block. There was a lot more to him than money and sexual charisma—she knew that—but everything was in such a muddle in her head she couldn't get the words out straight.

The newspapers often referred to Damon Gavros as 'educated muscle', with the recommendation that no one should even *dream* of crossing him—which was a great thought to say goodnight on.

His phone rang and he turned away to answer, putting a hand up, indicating two minutes as they stood outside the door.

'Business call,' he explained succinctly when he cut the line. 'So, I guess I'll see you again sometime…'

After all her prevaricating about seeing him at all, she now felt rocked to her foundations as Damon mounted the Harley and roared away. She *had* to see him again. She *must*. She stared after him as he disappeared into the night. That was Damon. A massive presence when he was around, and then gone so quickly it was as if he had never been there at all.

She did well to rely on no one but herself, Lizzie thought as she turned back to the restaurant.

But could there be a more mesmeric sight than Damon Gavros astride a Harley?

Damon Gavros naked…?

CHAPTER FOUR

LIZZIE, LIZZIE, LIZZIE... What are you hiding?

As he opened the door to his Thames-side pent-house flat Damon was still brooding. It had been shock enough to see Lizzie Montgomery again. To discover he could still read her as he had eleven years ago was even more unsettling—because he knew there was something she wasn't telling him.

He'd called in at the apartment to pick up his over-night bag. It was his father's seventieth birthday in a couple of weeks and his PA had called to remind him that Damon's go-ahead was still required for number of arrangements. They included a rather special youth orchestra from London that had been booked to play at his father's birthday party.

Too many loose ends had been generated by his absence abroad, Damon reflected as the driver took his bag. Lizzie had briefly derailed his plans, but they were back on track now. He'd like to see her again, but she'd have to fly out to the island. He'd fix it with Stavros, and his PA would make the arrangements.

That was how simple things were for him. He saw no reason for them to change.

As usual, Lizzie could hardly get a word in. She was meeting Thea for their daily snatched chat over brunch in a café just across the road from the music college, and today Thea was particularly excited.

'The new Gavros building is right next door to the music conservatoire,' Thea was enthusing. 'You should *see* it. Everything's been changed around and made super deluxe since that boring insurance company owned it.'

And the Gavros building was as dangerously close to the music conservatoire as it could possibly be Lizzie realised as she called for the bill. She hated it that the tension generated by the Gavros name was threatening to distract her from this precious time with Thea, but she had to find out more.

'You've been inside the Gavros building?' Her heart hammered nineteen to the dozen as she waited for Thea's answer.

'Of course!' Thea enthused, sucking gloopy milk from her fingers. 'We had to audition for the man—'

Lizzie's heart dived into her throat. 'What man? Was he tall and dark?'

'No. Short, fat and bald,' Thea said—to Lizzie's relief. 'He said he worked for the Gavros family. We're playing at a birthday party in Greece, on an island owned by the Gavros family.'

The Gavros family?

Thea glanced up as Lizzie inhaled sharply. Lizzie

quickly distracted Thea with talk of new clothes. 'You'll need a sunhat, a swimming costume, and perhaps a couple of sundresses—What?' She laughed as Thea mimed thrusting her fingers down her throat whilst gargling theatrically.

'Sundresses are for old ladies,' Thea insisted. 'And *you* need new clothes more than me,' she added with engaging honesty. She frowned. 'You *are* coming to Greece to hear us play, aren't you?'

'Of course I am,' Lizzie confirmed, her stomach clenching with alarm as she thought about it. 'I haven't missed a concert yet, have I?'

'Good.' Thea relaxed.

Lizzie's concerns about the Gavros family would have to be put to one side. She'd take *any* job to pay her way. Practical considerations—like where the money for her airfare would come from—were secondary to Lizzie's determination that she would do whatever it took to support Thea.

'Do you know whose birthday party it is?' she asked casually as they went up to the counter to pay the bill.

'Some old gentleman, I think,' Thea said vaguely, clearly not too interested.

It didn't *have* to be Damon's father. *Thea's grandfather.*

Lizzie's stomach clenched tight. Sucking in a breath, she jumped straight in. 'You know we never talk about your father—'

'Because we don't need to,' Thea cut across her, frowning. 'And I don't *want* to,' she added stubbornly. 'Why do I need a father when I've got you?'

'It might be nice to—'

'Ha!' Thea exclaimed dismissively. 'We don't even know where he is. He's probably on the other side of the planet.'

'What if I *did* know?'

'But you don't,' Thea insisted. 'And if you talked to my friends at school about parents at war you wouldn't be so keen to look for him either.'

'Not *all* marriages are like that.'

'Just most of them,' Thea said confidently. 'And we're happy, aren't we? Why would you want anything to change?'

'But what if things *did* change?' Lizzie tried gently.

'I'd change them back again.'

Thea sounded as confident as Lizzie had once been. And now their precious time together was up, Lizzie realised. She had to go to work and Thea had to go to school.

'We'll talk again,' she promised.

'In Greece,' Thea reminded her.

'In Greece,' Lizzie confirmed as she raised her umbrella to shelter them both.

Organising his father's party was a welcome change from Damon's usual work. He was enjoying it far more than he'd expected to. The high spirits of the volunteers was heartening. Everyone wanted to do their bit for the man who had done so much for them. Damon's father was universally loved. He'd brought prosperity to the island, and now he'd retired and passed the baton on, Damon was determined to do the same for those who had remained loyal to his father.

They would do more events like this, he decided. Mixing with good people had reminded him that not everyone was a fraudster or a gold-digger.

As he'd learned during the course of his meteoric rise, massive wealth brought vultures flocking, and they came in all shapes and sizes. Which was the only reminder he needed that what he'd seen in Lizzie eleven years ago had been the possibility for something more. He looked forward to his plans where Lizzie was concerned coming to fruition. And Stavros had proved a staunch ally.

The setting for his father's concert couldn't be bettered, he concluded as he walked across the sugar sand beach. An open-air stage had been erected on the playing fields behind the school where the youth orchestra were staying. The orchestra was already here and rehearsing and, like everyone else within earshot, he'd been entranced by their music.

One particular young livewire, with black bubbly curls and mischievous eyes, had just played the most extraordinary solo. She was the young violin prodigy everyone was talking about. She wasn't self-conscious or inflated by her success, as she might have been. She just loved her music—as Thea had told him.

He smiled as he remembered her explaining, 'Thea's a Greek name. I'm a bit Greek.'

He'd laughed. 'I'm a bit Greek too,' he'd told her.

'No. You're *all* Greek,' she'd argued, staring up

at him intently. 'I can tell that from the colour of your eyes.'

'Is that such a bad thing?'

'No. It's a very *good* thing,' she'd assured him. 'My mother's half-Greek, and my grandmother was all-Greek. I'm a bit Greek because I choose to be. You should meet my mother,' she'd added, squinting against the sun as she studied his face.

'Should I?' Another matchmaker, he'd thought, groaning inwardly.

But this matchmaker was different, he thought, remembering Thea's dramatically mournful expression as she'd explained, 'My mother's young, and very beautiful, and she's all alone.'

'Tragic,' he'd agreed, playing along. 'But I'm sure that if she's anything like you she won't be alone for long.'

After which he'd thought he should extricate himself as diplomatically as possible. Thea might have the makings of a great matchmaker, but he wasn't looking for a match.

Stavros had saved Lizzie. His cousin had a beach restaurant on the island owned by the Gavros family, and his cousin just happened to be desperate for more staff…according to Stavros.

Another coincidence? Or not?

Lizzie had known she couldn't afford to be picky when Stavros had adopted a dreamy expression as he'd described the island of his birth, adding, 'You haven't heard from Damon, I suppose?'

'No,' Lizzie had admitted, thinking it better to break it to him that, sooner rather than later, that Cupid had failed. 'And I don't expect to.'

So here she was, standing outside Cousin Iannis's restaurant, on what looked and sounded like a party night. She was feeling optimistic. How could she not, when Thea had called to say she had settled in and everything was going really well, and she'd made a lot of new friends on the island?

It was hard not to fall in love with the island, Lizzie thought as she stared up at the star-peppered sky. It was warm even this late at night, and the candles glowing inside the restaurant gave everything such a welcoming glow. Traditional music was playing, and the scent of delicious food made her hungry.

Iannis had picked her up at the airport, and now he ushered her inside and directed her towards the kitchen.

'We're in training for the big birthday party next week,' he explained above the din of crashing plates and shouts of, *'Oopa!'*

Iannis was the double of his cousin Stavros, and Lizzie doubted either man needed an excuse to hold a party. They were both kindness personified. Stavros had insisted on paying for her flight, saying he owed her holiday money, and now there was this— the warmest of welcomes.

'No work tonight!' Iannis insisted as she glanced at the row of servers' aprons hanging on pegs in the lobby outside the kitchen. 'You've only just arrived, so tonight you're my guest at the party. Your apartment is just up those stairs by the entrance door—' he indicated where '—and your luggage is already on its way up to your room.'

'You're too kind.'

'No. *You're* too kind,' Iannis argued. 'Stavros has told me all about you—and he has insisted that I mustn't work you too hard. No buts,' he warned. 'Your time here is to be a holiday. It's all arranged.'

Flinging the door to the kitchen wide, he ushered Lizzie in to meet his staff.

She froze on the threshold. 'Damon?'

What was he doing here?

Leaning back against the wall, looking as hot as sin, Damon raised a brow and smiled faintly as she walked in.

'Are you stalking me?' she challenged lightly.

'Surely it's the other way around?' he countered in his low, husky drawl.

She was instantly tense, thinking of Thea just a few miles down the road.

'Lizzie?' Damon pressed.

He was instantly suspicious. 'Damon,' she replied coolly.

Lifting her chin, she met his stare steadily. Pulses of heat rushed through her. He was so unbelievably good-looking, and she needed thinking time. She should have known he would be on the island— after all, his family owned it—but somehow she'd just blanked the possibility from her mind.

'Is something distracting you?' he asked.

Oh, so much! 'The sight of such delicious food,' she lied.

He looked at her as if he didn't believe a word of it. 'It certainly is a distraction.'

'I didn't expect to see you,' she admitted.

He raised a brow, and his eyes burned with amusement as his gaze roved openly over the outline of her body beneath her jeans and simple top. She would have said something, but with Iannis looking on with interest she knew that wouldn't be wise. She hated to disappoint her matchmakers, and she wouldn't be rude in front of them, but neither Iannis nor Stavros knew her history with Damon. And nor would they, if *she* had anything to do with it.

'Damon has been working all day to make things special for my staff,' Iannis explained. 'We are catering the big birthday party next week.'

That was all she needed to know. Why else would Damon be here if it weren't for the fact that it was his father's birthday they were talking about?

'He wanted my people to have a night off,' Iannis was explaining proudly.

Lizzie quickly pulled herself together. 'That's very good of him,' she agreed.

'And as soon as you've settled in you must come down to the party,' Iannis insisted. 'That's right, isn't it, Damon?' he pressed.

'Most definitely,' Damon confirmed, with a look at Lizzie that sucked the breath clean out of her lungs.

'Eat—drink—dance—make love!' Iannis exclaimed helpfully, with a wide smile. 'That's all that's allowed tonight.'

So long as they weren't all compulsory, Lizzie thought, while Damon's wicked smile reached his eyes and stayed there.

'Oh, and there are some gifts waiting for you on the bed upstairs,' Iannis added.

'Gifts for *me*?' Lizzie glanced at Damon.

'They're nothing to do with me,' he said.

So gifts from whom? Lizzie wondered.

'I'll see you downstairs as soon as you've had chance to freshen up,' Damon called after her as she left the kitchen.

She turned at the door. 'I'm not sure I'll be coming down again.'

'Of course you will.'

He said this in a way that made her run up the stairs as if the hounds of hell were after her.

Closing the door on her apartment, she closed her eyes and sucked in a deep, steadying breath. Damon only had to look at her for lust to surge through her veins, and that was dangerous. She was a very different person now from the girl she'd been at eighteen. She had far more sense, Lizzie told herself firmly as she switched on the light and looked around.

The first thing she saw were the 'gifts' laid out on the bed. She knew immediately who they were from, and rushed across the room to pick the dresses up and hold them to her face. Then she reached for her phone.

'Sundresses for the old lady!' she said, laughing happily as Thea came on the line.

Thea giggled. 'Do you like them?'

'I love them—but you shouldn't be spending your money on me.'

'I bought them at the market on our first day here. As soon as I saw them I knew I had to buy them for you. I fell in love with the sunny yellow one right away, and the blue's so pretty.'

'I love them both,' Lizzie admitted. She would never have wasted her scant funds on buying anything so frivolous for herself.

'Do they fit?' Thea demanded.

'They're perfect.' Hugging the dresses close, she battled to contain her emotions.

'Be sure to wear one of them for the concert.'

'I will,' Lizzie promised. 'I'll see you tomorrow. I can't wait to hear you play.'

'Playing the violin isn't *everything*,' Thea informed Lizzie, stalling her thoughts in a way that had never happened before.

'What do you mean?' Lizzie asked, wondering if she'd said or done something to discourage Thea.

'Just that. Love's far more important than anything else,' Thea explained loftily. 'Love is all I care about now. I'm in a romantic phase.'

'I see...' Lizzie said faintly.

She didn't see at all. Instead she wondered if she'd ruined two people's lives now.

She had to stop this, Lizzie accepted. She was always feeling guilty about something, and she had done so since her father's trial. As soon as she had discovered how many innocent people he'd harmed, and thought about the many expensive gifts he'd bought for her over the years, she had been plagued with guilt until it had become part of her psyche.

'Gotta go,' Thea said, startling Lizzie back into the moment. 'I'll send you a text!'

'Bye, sweetheart…'

She was the luckiest woman on earth, Lizzie thought, smiling as she stared at the small screen filled with kisses. She was so lucky to have Thea in her life, and she would never take that joy for granted.

The joy in which Damon should be sharing?

CHAPTER FIVE

GUILT HAD SNUFFED out Lizzie's happiness. She hated deception above all things. It was too strong a reminder of her father's betrayal. But the rules still applied. She *had* to tell Thea before Damon. And she couldn't just blurt it out down the phone. Thea had to be warned first...prepared. It would have to be done with the utmost sensitivity, and it was hard to find enough time to do that with a child who was always rehearsing.

Clinging to practicalities—as she always did when she couldn't see her way ahead clearly—Lizzie explored her small apartment. It was such a luxury to have all this space after the confines of her tiny bedsit back in London. The walls were simply whitewashed, and the floor was polished wood. There was a small kitchen at one end, with a fridge thoughtfully stocked with essentials, and a balcony where she could eat breakfast overlooking the sea. The bed looked big and felt comfy, and it had a lovely sky-blue throw at the foot that matched the rug on the floor... All the colours of Greece.

So, had she finished procrastinating? Was she going to freshen up now and go downstairs to see Damon?

Of course she was. Soon…

She spotted a local bus timetable amongst some magazines. She'd need those times for when she went to the school tomorrow to hear Thea play…

Glancing at her watch, she knew she couldn't put it off any longer. So, heading to the bathroom, she stripped off and took a shower. Turning her face up to the refreshing spray, she hugged herself and thought of Damon… Damon holding her… Damon kissing her… Damon making love to her—

She had to forget about it!

Forget Damon making love to her when he was in the same building, downstairs?

And another thing—if she didn't tell him about Thea soon he'd find out for himself.

Thea first and then Damon.

It seemed a long time ago since she'd discovered she was pregnant with Thea, and now every second seemed to be flying past, Lizzie thought as she towelled down.

On an impulse, she chose to wear one of the sundresses Thea had bought. She smiled when she put it on and felt better immediately. There was a lot of truth behind Thea's statement. Love was all that mattered. Sometimes Lizzie wished she could see life as clearly as a child. One thing was certain. She had to right this wrong.

Putting it off over the years had a lot to do with the

heartache she'd felt when her father had rejected her. Add to that her fear of losing Thea, and Lizzie would be the first to admit that she was just plain scared. She had always met problems head-on before, but the problems had never carried such a risk before.

Where *was* she? He shot another impatient look towards the stairs. His work was done. The second shift of people in his team had just arrived to take over the work in the kitchen. He was determined that Iannis and his staff would have a wonderful evening to thank them for all the work to come. He and his team had made sure of it. There was no reason for him to stick around.

No reason except Lizzie.

'Leaving so soon?'

His stare flashed up. Lizzie's comment had surprised him. She was calling to him from the top of the stairs.

He rested his fist on the wall. 'And if I am...?'

She shrugged. Her face was in shadow, so he couldn't see her expression. 'If you want to go—go. I won't hold you to your promise'

As she came slowly down the stairs her wildflower scent assaulted his senses. Her hair was still a little damp, and was hanging in tight curls, and her face was make-up-free. She was wearing a pretty sundress that exposed her pale, fragile skin and clung lovingly to the outline of her breasts. She had teamed this with simple sandals.

The punch to his senses was extraordinary. She

eclipsed all the society beauties he'd dated put together. His body responded accordingly, and it took all his willpower to rein it in.

He'd wasted a lot of time dating women who made no demands on him and barely scratched the surface of his interest. Lizzie was different. She'd always been different. She was the one woman who intrigued him, who made him want to know more.

'Are we going to stand here in the passage?' she asked him as people squeezed past.

'After you,' he invited.

He watched her walk ahead of him, small and proud, pale and sexy, with her striking red hair bouncing freely around her shoulders like a shimmering cloak of fire. The desire to grab a hank of that hair in his fist, so he could kiss her neck and see if that tiny tattoo of a tiger cub was still there, was overwhelming.

His libido badly needed a break, he concluded as they joined the couples dancing between the tables.

The next moment she had turned to face him and her arms were wrapped around him.

'What?' he murmured, staring down.

'Are we going to dance, or are we just going to stand here?'

He'd forgotten nothing.

'I'm glad you didn't leave,' she admitted as he took her hand in his.

She held his stare levelly, as if she wanted to say something but couldn't quite put it into words. There was something driving her to be with him, to stay with him, but if it wasn't sex what could it be?

'I think we'd better dance,' he agreed. The urge to feel her pressed up against him was irresistible.

'If you're brave enough.' She laughed.

'I've never flinched from a pair of sandals in my life.'

She looked at him and almost smiled openly, frankly, as she had eleven years ago, but she looked away as they began to move. She didn't need to hold his stare for them both to know that the contact between them was electric.

They were just relaxing into the rhythm when a band of partygoers crashed into the restaurant from the beach, performing a no-holds-barred version of the Conga.

Letting go of him, Lizzie pressed back against the wall to let the line of whooping dancers through. They stared at each other when they could as the seemingly endless line of bodies passed between them. Lizzie shrugged as it went on and on. He smiled ruefully. The wait seemed interminable, but finally the last of the revellers went by and, reaching out, he linked their fingers.

No other woman came close to making him feel this way, he thought as he slowly drew her towards him, and when every part of them was touching as they danced he knew he'd missed her even more than he could say.

She only had to hold Damon's hand and feel his other hand settle in the small of her back for nuclear explosions to be set off inside her. How could she have forgotten how good it felt to be this close to him? If only life weren't so complicated, she thought as he greeted old friends with warmth and good humour.

She had to get real, Lizzie accepted. Life *was* that complicated. Damon was a billionaire. She was nothing and no one. She could either enjoy this interlude for what it was, or invite trouble back into her life.

It was all very well, coming up with these good reasons for remaining detached, but when Damon drew her close and his hands became seductive spells she started trembling with awareness. She hated herself for being so weak, but she couldn't do anything about it. He *had* to feel how she responded to him— he must.

He did, Lizzie realised as her pulse went off the scale. The dark humour in Damon's eyes was all the proof she needed.

And then the band slowed the tempo and the music grew seductive. The melody wrapped a cord around her heart and pulled it tight. Music could always strip her emotions bare. She might not be a musician, like her mother or like Thea, but she responded as they did, and the plangent tune was currently ripping chunks out of her heart.

As if he sensed this, Damon tightened his arms around her, and in spite of all her sensible reservations she went to him as willingly as a boat slipping into its mooring. Her body burned with heat as he linked their fingers, bringing them to rest on his chest where she could feel his heart beating.

This was as close as two people could be without

making love. Her body was floating in an erotic net. She was made of sensation. Her worries dwindled as reality faded away. She had often daydreamed of being reunited with Damon, but this was so much better than her dreams.

If she closed her eyes the years melted away and she could think herself back into his bedroom, where whispers and touches had been magic spells and the smallest shift of Damon's fingers had delivered messages only she had been able to read. She wanted that back. She wanted to recapture the trust they'd shared for that one night. But would Damon ever trust her again when he learned about Thea? And could she blame him?

'Tense again?' he said. 'What's wrong now?'

When Damon stared into her eyes it was impossible to lie to him. 'You,' she said. 'It's time I went to bed. It's been a long day. Thanks for the dance.'

He caught hold of her hand. 'You can't leave it like that.'

'I just did. The mood is wrong. Too many people.'

'Sounds serious,' he said.

'It will keep.' *She hoped.* As her secret had been kept for eleven years, she had to believe it would keep a little longer.

She had already danced with Damon far longer than she'd had intended. But the band worked against her, segueing into another tune, allowing Damon to bring her close again.

Allowing? How hard did she fight him?

How could someone so much bigger than she was

hold her close and prove they fitted together perfectly? Just for a few moments she allowed herself to close her eyes and rest her cheek against his chest. It felt so good. His thigh brushed against her intimately—*by accident*, she told herself firmly. She was so on edge she was ready to believe anything.

He'd been tender and gentle on that night, as well as hot as hell and sexy, and sometimes she longed for that tenderness and intimacy of thought as much as the sexual act. She wanted that too, of course. She was a normal, healthy woman, and it was impossible to be this close to Damon without thinking about sex.

That night had drawn them closer than either might have expected. He'd confided his hopes for the future, his love for his family, and his desire one day to have a family of his own. She'd told him about the holidays she remembered having as a child, when her mother had been alive. Summers had seemed to last for ever then, and Lizzie's life had been full of warmth and a love she'd thought would go on for ever.

And then had come the hollow black part. She hadn't burdened him with that. And then the greatest gift of all—Thea. Motherhood. Responsibility. Love. She'd embraced all three with gratitude, but if life had taught her one thing it was never to take anything for granted.

'If I didn't know you better I'd say you had a guilty conscience,' Damon commented when she shifted restlessly in his arms.

'No guilt,' she said.

'Not even a tiny bit?'

She chose not to answer that. Of *course* there was guilt. There was more than one parent in Thea's life. How much *more* guilty could she feel?

Damon had often wondered if that first scorching spark between them would stand the test of time, and here was his answer. Sensation ruled him when Lizzie was in his arms. No other woman could come close to making him feel the way she did. His body was a raging conflagration of lust.

But what he liked best about her was her honesty. When other women would tell him what they thought he wanted to hear, Lizzie told him the truth, uncaring of the consequences. The temptation to kiss her—to kiss every part of her—was overwhelming, but once he started he wouldn't stop, and this was neither the right place nor the right time.

'Maybe you *should* go to bed now,' he agreed. Releasing her, he stood back. 'Alone,' he murmured when she stared up at him.

How had she allowed things to go this far? Lizzie wondered. At this moment in time she would have followed Damon to Hades and back. The thought of parting from him and going upstairs to bed held no appeal at all, yet just a few minutes ago she had known it was the only sensible thing to do.

Iannis intervened, moving between them and insisting on shepherding them to his table.

'The night isn't over yet,' he declared. 'Eat! Drink! I have reserved two places at my table—'

How could they let him down?

'Stavros would never forgive me if I allowed his favourite couple to miss out on the best part of the party—my food,' Iannis explained proudly.

Lizzie thought Damon very restrained in not mentioning that it was *his* people who'd cooked tonight. More importantly, they weren't a couple, as both Stavros and Iannis seemed to think. There was only Damon Gavros, billionaire, and Lizzie Montgomery, single mother with a child to protect.

'And now we dance the *kalamatianos*!' Iannis announced when the most delicious feast had been consumed.

He made a signal and a chord rang out. All his guests wanted to join in the famous national dance, and there was a group exodus from the tables.

'As my honoured guest, you shall have the honour of leading the dance,' he told Lizzie, handing her the traditional white handkerchief to hold aloft.

Her mother had taught her the steps of the dance when Lizzie was a child. They had often danced it together, with her mother humming the tune and Lizzie waving a little handkerchief over her head.

'If you'd rather not…?' Damon murmured.

'Try and stop me,' Lizzie said, standing up.

The distinctive twang of the bouzouki was like a rallying call. The rhythm, starting slowly and building up, made each Greek heart swell with longing. Waving the white handkerchief, Lizzie was the Pied

Piper, drawing her flock to the area in front of the restaurant where the beach met the land beyond.

'I'd kick off your sandals,' Damon advised.

He was doing the same, she noticed. How ridiculous to find his feet sexy. She had to stop this *now*. One more dance and then she was definitely going to bed.

It was as if a lightning bolt zapped through her when Damon seized one end of the white handkerchief, effectively joining them by a shred of cloth. Lizzie tightened her grip as Damon's heat seemed to invade the fabric, scorching her fingers, travelling on from there to her heart—

Really?

She was tired. Her mind was inventing things. They were dancing and that was all. But it wasn't just dancing, and it wasn't just music, it was memories wrapped up in a tune: a little girl dancing with her mother, holding her hand and believing that life would stay the same for ever.

'Lizzie…?' Damon murmured with concern.

Her eyes had filled with tears, she realised, dashing them away. 'Why do you have to notice *everything*?' she demanded impatiently.

The music suddenly picked up pace, forcing all the dancers to watch their feet rather than chat to their companions. Arms stretched out and resting on each other's shoulders, their cries of *'Oopa!'* grew louder, and as the dancing grew wilder several couples collapsed on the ground, laughing. But the band didn't stop.

Soon it was Lizzie's turn to grow dizzy, but as she

stumbled Damon's lightning reflexes saved her. 'I'm going to show you the island tomorrow,' he said as he steadied her on her feet.

She glanced at him in surprise. 'You can spare the time?'

He'd never looked more dangerous, she thought, and he was waiting. Decisions had to be made. Common sense told her to stay away from him, but getting to know him all over again took precedence.

'I'd have to ask Iannis.'

'*Would* you?' he flashed.

They both knew Iannis was only too keen to keep his part of the bargain with his cousin, and give Lizzie as much free time as possible.

'Maybe a couple of hours?' she said.

'Good. That's settled.'

'But I'd have to be back by two,' she said, remembering Thea's concert in the afternoon.

'That's no problem for me,' Damon assured her.

'Then, thank you. What time in the morning?'

'Eight. And bring a picnic.'

'Don't you have flunkies to do that for you?'

'They're away with my butler at the moment.'

Damon smiled, a flash of strong white teeth against his swarthy skin. She couldn't match it. Things were moving too fast.

She tried telling herself that if he could be as relaxed as this when he learned about Thea things would be okay, but she knew it wouldn't be that simple.

CHAPTER SIX

SHE HAD TRIED to get hold of Thea the next day, before she set off with Damon, but Thea had been having breakfast before an early rehearsal for the afternoon concert. And now Lizzie was out of touch, clinging to a handrail on board Damon's powerboat as they crashed through breakers as high as houses on the open sea.

He was full of surprises. The value of his air, sea, and land craft alone would fund a small country, with change to spare. He was standing at the helm, controlling the massive craft with one hand, as casually as if its immense power was just another extension of his magic.

He looked more like a marauding brigand than a respectable billionaire, with his swarthy skin and unshaven face, she thought, taking in the ripped and faded shorts, his bare feet and faded top.

'Have you never been on a powerboat before?' he asked as she lurched towards him.

'The closest I've come to this is the cross-Channel ferry.'

'Then it's time to widen your horizons.'

She murmured in reply. She'd tried that once before, and now she preferred to limit her horizons to Thea.

'So, where are we going?' she asked. 'No—don't turn to look at me!' she yelped as Damon swung round. 'Shouldn't you be concentrating on where you're going?'

He laughed. 'I know *exactly* where I'm going.'

Yes. That was what she was afraid of, and she only wished she felt half so confident as Damon looked.

Having rebuilt her life, Lizzie controlled it within certain boundaries, but those boundaries seemed to be disappearing fast. Telling Thea about Damon and then explaining to Damon that he had a daughter had seemed so straightforward in the planning, but time was rushing past and she seemed no further on.

'Is this our destination?' she asked as he slowed the powerboat. It was beautiful. She stared around with interest at the picturesque bay.

'It's called Cove Krýstallo,' Damon explained. 'Or Crystal Cove. This area has always been a favourite of mine on the island, and now I've built a house here.'

And not just a house but the most magnificent dwelling Lizzie had ever seen, she thought as he eased back on the throttle. The mansion was built of blush-pink stone. Low built, to blend in with its surroundings, it was elegant and vast. It could be called a beach house, she supposed, because of its seafront position, but it was a beach house fit for a billionaire.

She was so far out of the customary modest rut that she shared with Thea, it was becoming ridiculous.

'We'll be back for two. I haven't forgotten,' Damon said as she frowned and shook her head with incredulity.

'Thanks.' She supposed she should be grateful that he couldn't read her mind.

As he turned away to lower the anchor she took stock. Apart from her anxiety at being introduced to yet another example of Damon's incredible wealth, the consequences of being alone with him in this secluded bay were finally coming home to her. It didn't help when a rogue wave crashed against the hull and she lost her balance, cannoning into him. As he steadied her his touch woke memories better forgotten.

She pulled away self-consciously and was glad when he made a joke of it.

'Lost your sea legs?' he suggested, staring at her with amusement.

'I don't think I ever had any.'

She could still feel his touch, where his hand had lingered on her shoulder, and feel the heat created when he had stared into her eyes.

There was no point in aching for something she could never have back, Lizzie told herself firmly. And why would she *want* it back? The last time she'd had sex with Damon he'd enjoyed it, and then had cut loose and disappeared. Only Thea had made that night more than worthwhile.

Thea had made Lizzie's life incalculably richer, while Damon had played no part in her life aside from that one night. And she wasn't eighteen now, twisting her mother's dying wish for Lizzie to have a better and more adventurous life into an excuse to have sex with Damon here in his private cove.

'Race you to shore?' he suggested, straightening up after checking the anchor was safely attached to the seabed.

'Do you need a head start?' she suggested, straight-faced. It wasn't too far to shore, and she was confident of her abilities in the water.

He laughed, and the ache of longing inside her increased.

'I'll give you a ten-minute head start,' he offered, with the same deadpan expression.

'You'll be sorry,' she warned with a laugh.

She was wearing a bikini beneath her shorts and top, and quickly stripped off.

Damon's look scorched over her. Ignoring how that made her feel, she climbed onto the rail, telling herself that if ever there had been a need for the re-freshing shock of chilly water, this was it.

She caught a glimpse of Damon's half-smile as he watched her dive in. She also saw the power in his thighs and in his shoulders and back, and the taut out-line of his buttocks beneath his faded denim shorts.

The next thing she knew she was shrieking with excitement as she surfaced. The all-embracing chill of the ocean after the balmy warmth on deck was just the reboot she needed. Kicking off strongly, she headed for the shore, with no thought in her head other than to get there before him.

She trod water to look back, only to see him clos-ing in fast. She set off again, with the excitement of

the chase driving her now. She was a strong swim-
mer, and competitive, but even with the waterproof
pack containing their picnic to hamper him Damon
was slicing through the water like an arrow. He soon
passed her, and only slowed when he'd reached the
shallows, where he stood and turned to watch her
power in.

'Not bad,' he commented. 'But I'll carry you the
rest of the way.'

'You will *not*,' she protested and, finding her feet,
stood up.

She shrieked in complaint as Damon ignored her
and swung her into his arms.

'Put me down,' she said, pummelling him as she
struggled to break free. It was like beating her fists
against rock.

'If I put you down you'll cut your feet on the
shells,' he said.

'And you've got hooves?' she shot back.

He laughed.

She'd forgotten how strong he was. Fighting him
only brought her into more intimate contact with him.
But still she couldn't give up. 'I'm not a baby, Damon.
Put me down—'

'And I'm not a nursemaid to waste my time ban-
daging your feet.'

Thwarted, she went as stiff as a board and tried
her best not to relax against him. It wasn't so easy
to forget the last time Damon had carried her like
this—which had been out of his shower and back to
bed on the morning of her father's trial. They'd made

love again, and then he'd told her he had an appointment to keep.

She'd thought nothing of it at the time...until she'd seen him in the courtroom. If she'd learned one thing from that experience, it was that Damon could be ruthless.

He put her down on the cool, damp, close-knit moss above the shoreline. Dropping the waterproof pack on the ground, he helped her to set out their picnic.

When that was done, she sat back and leaned on her elbows with her face turned to the sky.

'Penny for them?' he asked as she sighed.

'I was just thinking that it's very beautiful here,' she said, inhaling deeply as a cover for the fact that her thoughts, having travelled back to that night and that morning, and all the mixed emotions that had filled her eleven years ago, were refusing to settle down again.

'It *is* very beautiful,' he agreed, coming to sit at her side. 'Lucky for you Iannis could put you up,' he commented. 'What made you think of coming to this island in the first place?'

Lizzie's eyes flashed open. She was instantly on high alert. 'Stavros suggested it,' she said quickly. 'I'm very lucky to have such good friends.'

'You are,' he agreed. 'And it appears that fate is determined to throw us together.'

She huffed out a short laugh as Damon glanced at her. She couldn't read his expression, but she knew enough to be wary. 'Bad luck for both of us, I guess.'

'If you say so,' he murmured. Knocking the top

off a bottle of beer, he brought it to his lips. 'Whatever made you come here, you should take the chance to relax while you can. What have you got to lose?'

Everything, Lizzie thought as Damon drank deep.

Putting the beer down, he rested his chin on his knee and studied her face. 'I'm glad you got rid of the lip ring.'

She touched her lip, feeling faintly affronted. 'That was a long time ago.'

'You've changed a lot,' he agreed.

'Eleven years.' She shrugged. 'What did you expect?'

Damon's lips pressed down, but he didn't answer.

'Why didn't you like my lip ring?' she asked, frowning.

'Because it got in the way when I kissed you.'

'That isn't...' Heat ripped through her when Damon leaned in.

'Isn't what?' he said. 'Fair?'

'Sensible,' she said as he curved her a smile.

'Sensible?' he mocked, sitting back. 'Is that what you are now?'

'No one stays eighteen for ever, Damon.'

'No,' he agreed. 'But whatever age you are you can still live and feel and dare.'

'Oh, I *dare*,' Lizzie assured him, angling her chin to stare him in the eyes. 'I just don't want to be hurt again.'

'Hurt?' He frowned. 'Do you expect me to hurt you?'

'I just know I won't give you the chance.'

'It was *you* who stormed off,' he pointed out.

She couldn't deny it. She had, Lizzie remembered.

'Are you going storm off now?' he asked.

'As I said, I'm not eighteen.'

'No. You're much improved.'

The smile behind his eyes had just become dangerous. Being this close to him was dangerous enough, without that hard mouth teasing her with a faint smile. Her sensible mind said, *Leave now, move away, make him take you back to the restaurant*. But it was hard to be sensible when she wanted him so much.

She'd only have to move by the smallest degree for their lips to touch, and for Damon's arms to close around her.

And then she did, and they did, and she was lost.

She was back.

The rush of triumph inside him was like nothing he'd ever known—not for eleven years, at least. She was everything he remembered and more, and she came to him as if their years apart had disappeared. She pressed against him, responding fiercely as he kissed her. She was strong and sure, and every bit his match.

Their tongues tangled as she clung to him, and when he eased her legs apart with his thigh she arced her body against his in the hunt for more contact. Cupping her buttocks with one hand, he unlaced the strings of her bikini with the other as they traded kisses hungrily.

Glancing down nearly wrecked his control. He was painfully and hugely erect, while Lizzie was as sen-

sitive as he remembered. He only had to stroke her
lightly to hear her purr. He parted her lips and found
the tiny bud. He teased and then pulled away, then
teased some more as she clung to him, gasping out
her pleasure.

'Beneath me now,' he instructed softly.

There was no need to ask. Lizzie was way ahead
of him.

'Slowly,' he advised as she bucked towards him.

'Why?' Her eyes challenged him.

'Because it's been a long time.'

She raised an amused brow. 'Like I don't remember?'

Neither of them could forget, it seemed. The mem-
ory of taking her, of sinking deep into Lizzie's tight,
moist heat, was seared on his brain for all time. Max-
imum control was essential as he prepared to redis-
cover the woman he had enjoyed like no other.

He stroked and kissed and took his time. Lizzie
was all hunger and need, and he had to slow her down.
Teasing her, he cupped her between the legs, denying
her the contact she wanted.

He smiled as he watched her eyes darken. 'I've got
you now,' he whispered.

'You think?' she whispered back.

'Shall we put it to the test?' he suggested, still teasing her with kisses.

'This is your island, and this is your beach, so I
guess you can do anything you like,' she said, seem-
ing pleased at this idea.

'Do you want me to?'

'What do you *think* I want you to do?'

He smiled as she moved restlessly beneath him.

Hearing foil rip, she lifted her hips, and she was so aroused that at his first intimate touch she was reaching greedily for release.

This was the Lizzie he remembered from eleven years ago. This was the woman with whom he'd made love on every surface in his apartment—including pressed up against the floor-to-ceiling windows, where anyone who'd wanted to could have seen.

'You're right,' he agreed. 'We—*you*,' he amended as he pinned her wrists above her head '—can do anything you want to do while you're here.'

'Including to you?' she said. 'Can I use you for my pleasure?'

'I don't see why not.' He grinned. 'But that would be for *my* pleasure too.' Pressing her knees back, he moved between them. 'Hold them for me.'

'Like this? So I'm exposed…?'

She sounded so excited.

He told her yes.

She did as he asked, and now her brown eyes were almost black, with just a rim of sepia around her pupils. She was right on the edge.

'Don't tease me,' she warned.

'Pleasure delayed is pleasure intensified,' he taunted softly.

'None of that rubbish now,' she warned him.

Taking hold of his arms, she arranged herself to her liking and shuddered out a soft cry when he gave her just the tip.

'What?' he murmured, sinking deeper.

'You...this...'

He rocked his hips forward and gave her a little more. He pulled out completely before sinking even deeper into her tight, warm grip. The pleasure was intense. It took everything he'd got to hold back so she could get used to the invasion. She was throbbing around him, insistently drawing him on. He only had to move the smallest fraction for her to wail and let go.

Helpless in the grip of violent release, she bucked frantically back and forth, while he held her in place, making sure that she benefited from every last pulse of pleasure.

'Worth the wait?' he murmured when she quietened.

She was still groaning rhythmically against his mouth as the pleasure pulses, having faded, continued. He started to move again and she immediately responded, moving with him, needing more.

Making love to Lizzie was instantly familiar all over again. He knew exactly what she needed, and it gave him the greatest pleasure to give it to her. The only change he noted was that her appetite had grown.

It was a long time later when he hauled her to her feet and they ran to cool down in the sea. He swung her into his arms both times, to avoid the shells, and when he carried her back to shore and they dressed she reminded him that they had to get back.

'An appointment?' he confirmed. 'I remember. Sadly no time for the house today.'

'Another time?' she said.

'Why not?' he agreed.

As they linked fingers to walk along the sand, to a soundtrack of rolling surf and seabirds calling, he wondered if he'd ever felt closer to anyone. Trust was a great thing, and he was glad he'd got Lizzie's back.

He was proud of her—not for that reason, but for the way she'd fought back after the trial. She'd barely spoken of it, but he knew she must have had a rough time. The spirit he remembered so well from eleven years back must have carried her through, and it was no wonder that Iannis and Stavros liked her so much, and Stavros had wanted her to come to the island.

Rediscovering her Greek heritage would be good for Lizzie. There was nothing like a return to the homeland for restoring confidence and faith in the future.

'Your new house is very beautiful,' she said, glancing over her shoulder. You must be very proud of it?'

'I am,' he admitted, 'especially as I had the pleasure of helping to build it.'

'That must have been great,' she agreed.

He was pleased that she understood the pleasure he'd found in working with his hands. 'It was,' he confirmed.

He glanced back too. Looking at his new place through Lizzie's eyes gave him the same thrill that he'd felt when he'd first sat back to study his design on paper. He'd planned for the house to be in complete harmony with its surroundings, and he believed he'd succeeded.

'It's fabulous,' Lizzie confirmed as they both paused to admire it.

'I did have some help,' he admitted dryly. But he felt the pleasure that only a man who'd selected each piece of stone from the quarry could feel. 'Without the craftsmen I employed it would never have been built. I worked as their lowly assistant.'

'That must have been a bit different for you,' she said, 'but from the look on your face I guess you enjoyed it?'

'More than you know,' he agreed.

'Well, it was well worth the effort. You've created something really beautiful.'

'*You're* beautiful,' he said, swinging her into his arms. 'And one day I will bring you back here.'

Would he? Lizzie wondered. Would Damon want her within a hundred miles of him when he found out the truth about Thea?

'Beautiful' didn't begin to describe his new home. It was a dream home. It was the type of home Lizzie wished she could give to Thea.

And Thea's father owned it.

Her mouth dried when she compared Damon's glorious beachside mansion to the one room she shared with Thea in London when Thea was home from school. How could she deny Thea this incredible lifestyle? Thea could have half a dozen music studios and no one would ever complain about the noise.

'You could paint here,' Damon said.

She swung around to stare at him in confusion for

a moment. Her head was so full of Thea, as it always was, that she couldn't switch track to herself.

'You used to love painting,' Damon prompted. 'I remember you telling me.'

'I did,' she agreed. Incredibly, on that night eleven years ago, they had grown close enough to discuss lots of things, including pastimes and hopes and dreams. 'You told me that work was *your* hobby,' she remembered.

'Correct,' Damon confirmed. 'And it still is.'

'I didn't have a clue what you meant by saying that back then,' she admitted. 'I'd only just left school and had no idea that the world could be so tough.'

And the rest, she thought.

And now you do? Damon's look said.

She didn't deserve the compassion in his eyes. Damon had been forced to become even more work-obsessed after the trial, thanks to the damage done to his family's business by her father. Damon had righted all those wrongs, but maybe life would have turned out differently for him if there'd been no fraud, no trial, and they had never met.

CHAPTER SEVEN

DAMON SEEMED DETERMINED to reassure her. 'It's good to have you back,' he commented as they walked on.

And good to have *you* back, Lizzie thought, though she knew better than to expect it to be for ever.

She lowered her gaze so Damon wouldn't be able to see how she felt about him.

'I was worried I'd lost you again,' he admitted. 'I'd keep seeing flashes of the old Lizzie, but then she'd slip away.'

There was a good reason for that, Lizzie thought, hanging back. 'You can't recapture time, or make it stand still, Damon.'

'But I can care that you were hurt,' he argued firmly. 'And I can care that I was partly responsible for causing that hurt. I can care that your father abandoned you, and your stepmother kicked you in the teeth when you had no one left to defend you—'

'I didn't need anyone to defend me. I was fine on my own—better, probably. I think we look at success differently, and I'm actually *pleased* with the way things have turned out.'

'How *can* you be?' he said frowning.

Thea was always front and foremost in her mind, and that left her nothing to complain about. 'When I once had such big dreams, do you mean? I see things differently now. I don't owe any money. I've got a roof over my head and enough food to eat.' And, more importantly, a daughter she adored, and Thea didn't go without anything if Lizzie could help it. 'You don't need to feel sorry for me,' she said with absolute certainty.

'I don't feel sorry for you. I *admire* you,' Damon insisted.

'Well, that sounds a little bit patronising.'

He seemed surprised. 'I apologise if you think that, because it's the last thing I intended. I *do* admire you, and I think it's great that you—'

'Survived?' she supplied edgily.

'I think you've done more than that, haven't you?' he argued. 'I was going to say that you've got great friends, and a life you enjoy, so nothing else should matter.'

'I'm glad you see it that way.' She was determined to move on to safer ground—which meant switching the spotlight to Damon. 'And *you've* done very well for yourself too,' she said dryly. 'Understatement,' she added with a grin.

His lips pressed down as he shrugged. 'I had a strong family behind me all the way. And I took over an existing business with an excellent reputation.'

That Lizzie's father had almost destroyed.

'Stop,' he warned, reading her. 'No one, least of

all me, blames you for your father's crimes. The only thing that *does* puzzle me,' he admitted, 'is that you always had what it took to get ahead, but for some reason it hasn't worked out for you as well as I expected. Obviously I'm curious to know why.'

She brushed his remark aside with a casual gesture, though everything inside her had tightened in a knot. 'I wouldn't waste your time investigating me.'

He huffed a laugh, but she didn't kid herself that this was over. Damon's interest in her life over the past eleven years had been well and truly stirred, and he wouldn't let go now. Nothing would satisfy him but a full explanation.

'In case you hadn't noticed,' he said in excuse, 'you interest me. No one had ever taken me on as you did outside that courtroom. You were only just eighteen and, apart from your fair-weather friends, you were on your own. I was older, surrounded by family and a legal team, but *nothing* stopped you. There's nothing wrong with asserting your rights and showing loyalty to your family—that's something I really get. You were right to stand your ground—and right to rage at me. I *was* a bastard.'

'You admit it?' Amusement cut through her anxiety for a few moments. 'Maybe there's hope for you yet.'

She should have known that Damon would take advantage of this lighter mood. He jumped straight on it.

'So, are you going to tell me what happened to the promises you made to yourself about developing your painting and your cooking, and all those other dreams?'

'What is it they say about promises?' she countered. 'Aren't they like pie crusts, made to be broken?'

Damon's gaze sharpened on her face. 'If there's one thing I won't believe it's that you gave up your dreams easily. There must be something big you're not telling me.'

'There is,' she agreed. 'It's called life.'

He looked at her sceptically.

'Life moves on, Damon, and we have to move with it.'

Eleven years of fighting, with her only goal being to make a good life for Thea. Her goal remained the same today, and it didn't allow for dreams.

'That's enough,' he declared, swinging her into his arms. 'I won't send you back with a frown on your face.

She laughed. It was such a relief to escape the dangerous topic.

Damon carried her across the shells to the sea so they could swim back to the boat. She exhaled raggedly when he set her down at the water's edge and his hands skimmed her breasts. She stared into his eyes, wondering if it was wrong to feel this happy, and if she'd be made to pay. If happiness was an indulgence she didn't deserve she was going to be in debt for the rest of her life, because she was drowning in the stuff.

She sucked in a breath as Damon's hands touched her breasts. 'Your breasts are fuller than I remember. And your nipples are a deeper, rosier pink—'

Pregnancy, she thought, immediately tensing. She was right not to count on happiness lasting. It hadn't even made it back to the boat.

'I'm older,' she dismissed with a shrug.

He huffed a laugh. '*So* old,' he agreed dryly, adding, 'You never could take a compliment, could you, Lizzie?'

As Damon stared into her eyes, as if searching for the truth he knew she was hiding, she grew increasingly anxious. 'What time is it?' she asked, worrying about Thea, worrying about Damon, worrying about everything…

'Time enough,' he soothed, running his fingertips down her cheek to her lips. 'We'll be back before two. We can see the house another time. I blame you for being so irresistible.'

As he took Lizzie's face between his hands he felt her tremble. His fingers ploughed into her hair, his thumbs caressed her jawbone just below her ears, but she couldn't be soothed and when he kissed her he felt tears on her face.

He blamed himself. He'd been so busy driving forward after the trial, trying to make everything right again for his father, that he hadn't spared a thought for Lizzie, and now he could only imagine what she'd been through.

'I'm sorry,' he whispered as her shoulders shook beneath his hands. 'This is my fault. The way I treated you was—'

'No. Please don't say that,' she argued fiercely.

'You're a *good* man, Damon. If your father hadn't spoken up mine would have destroyed even more people. I didn't want to see his faults then, but I can see them now.'

'We should get back,' he murmured.

'Yes,' she said, staring into his eyes.

Damon's kisses were drugging reminders of a time she would never forget. His body pressed against hers was a reminder her of how safe she felt in his arms. Fate was cruel—acting as if they were meant to be together, meant to have had Thea, meant to meet again in Stavros's restaurant and here on the island. Fate was taunting them, she suspected.

Damon pulled away first and glanced out to sea at the powerboat in a silent signal that their idyll was over. They both had to return to their lives and to reality, and to all the problems that lay ahead of them.

Lifting her chin, she said, 'I'm ready if you are.'

The first thing she did when they were back on the powerboat was check the clock, to make sure she would be in good time to catch the local bus to Thea's concert. She felt embarrassed when Damon caught her looking, and wondered if he thought she was trying to hurry the time away.

'Thank you,' she said softly.

He made a sound of acknowledgement, but there was plenty to do as he prepared the powerboat for leaving, and no more time for conversation. Not that there was anything left to say—not before she'd spoken to Thea.

* * *

He was frustrated by Lizzie's reluctance to admit that there was something troubling her. She trusted him enough to have sex with him, but not enough to allow him to help her. What could be *that* bad?

After eleven years he would have been more surprised if they *didn't* have things to tell each other, but if it was another man, and that was why she couldn't say anything, then she was no better than her father. He refused to believe that of her.

He should have asked her straight out—would have done if they had devoted more time to talking and less time to sex. He might expect the Greek community to close around her, but why hadn't Stavros said something? Why hadn't Iannis? Didn't *they* trust him either?

He respected their silence—he was forced to admit that. He just hated being in the dark, and apart from hearing third-hand while he was in the desert that Lizzie's father had died in prison, and that her stepmother was living with another man, he knew next to nothing about those eleven years where Lizzie was concerned.

They had an uneventful journey back to the other side of the island. They disembarked, exchanged the usual pleasantries, and then he drove her to the door of the restaurant. But everything had changed; she was tense now.

'Thank you,' she exclaimed with relief. 'You said you had somewhere to be too? I hope I haven't made you late?'

He shrugged. 'A visit to my parents' home to discuss the last-minute arrangements for my father's party can be delayed as long as it needs to be.'

She glanced at him with concern. 'You're sure?'

'Don't be late. Go,' he insisted.

'I can't thank you enough,' she said, turning to give him one last rabbit-in-the-headlights smile.

He ground his jaw at the knowledge that whatever had brought bold and feisty Lizzie back to him it had now, for reasons unknown, taken her away again.

He kept the engine purring in neutral long enough to see her disappear inside the restaurant, and then his phone rang just as he was about to drive away.

'No problem,' he told his father, who had asked if Damon would mind delaying their meeting.

'You can go and listen to the orchestra instead of me, and give me a report,' his father suggested.

'I'd love to,' he said dryly.

Maybe music could 'soothe a savage breast', he reflected, thinking about Lizzie and the secret she found so hard to share with him.

CHAPTER EIGHT

IANNIS HAD PROMISED Lizzie that she could set her watch by the local bus. And so it proved to be. She got off the bus outside the school grounds where Thea was due to play that afternoon with ample time to spare.

She took a moment to smooth her lovely yellow dress and her hair. Her old lady dress, Lizzie thought, smiling as she remembered what Thea had said. It was a beautiful dress, made all the more lovely by the thought behind it. It had been a long time since Lizzie had worn anything but jeans and a top, or a server's uniform, and she wanted Thea to know how much the gift of a dress meant to her.

The school was set in a picturesque valley between lush, vine-covered hills. It thrilled Lizzie to think that Thea's talent had brought her to such a beautiful place. Set like a jewel in an aquamarine sea, the island boasted shady olive groves and sparkling rivers and, though it was hot today, there was a covered awning to keep both audience and performers cool.

Nothing had been overlooked. Refreshments had been set out on trestle tables, and it promised to be a wonderful afternoon. Excitement gripped Lizzie as she anticipated another performance. This one was more of a rehearsal, and that, together with knowing that Damon was visiting his parents allowed her to relax and enjoy the fact that Thea Floros—as Thea was known now, having taken Lizzie's mother's name—would be the star soloist today.

Lizzie glowed with pride as she joined the line of parents waiting to take their seats. When at last the gates to the school opened and everyone filed in Lizzie only wished she were taller, so she could be the first to catch sight of Thea. For now she had to be content with shuffling along at a snail's pace, walled in by a platoon of parents, but then people finally started sitting down and she could see the children.

'Eísai entáxei. Megáli chaméni efkairía?'

'Are you all right?' someone translated for Lizzie as she swayed.

She caught hold of a nearby chair for support.

'It must be the heat,' she excused. 'I don't see this much sun in London, but thank you for your concern.'

The kindness of strangers couldn't help her now. How could Thea be talking to *Damon*? He wasn't supposed to be here. He was supposed to be visiting his parents. And Thea wasn't just *chatting* to him, as a child might talk politely to a stranger who had expressed an interest in her music, she was laughing with him as if they were old friends.

Two dark heads with the same thick, wavy black

hair. Two sets of laughing brown eyes. Two tanned faces with features so similar, so strong, and both so beautiful.

Thea had said something that had made Damon shove his hands into the back pockets of his jeans, throw his head back and laugh. Lizzie felt the chill of exclusion. What could they be saying to each other? How much did Damon know?

Worse! How much did *Thea* know?

She had never seen Damon looking so relaxed, or Thea so happy. Theirs was such an unexpected rapport it frightened her. It had always been just the two of them before. Thea and Lizzie... Lizzie and Thea. But now the likeness between father and daughter was startling.

Seeing them together for the first time was the most unnerving experience of Lizzie's life. It wasn't just that Damon's full-blooded Greek genes had prevailed over Lizzie's part-Greek, part-Celtic mix, but the fact was that anyone could see that Damon and Thea were father and daughter. Could Damon see it too? Could Thea?

She stood motionless, watching, numb with shock. It was too late to do anything properly now. The moment had come and gone, and watching Thea and Damon together stirred new fears. How quickly Lizzie's father had lost interest in her, once his life had changed. She'd been determined to protect Thea from that. But now she wondered if she'd been overprotective. Had she got everything wrong?

Both Damon and Thea had cause to hate her. And

she'd done that all on her own. Damon's first thought would be to protect Thea. Could she blame him for that? How could she, when Lizzie had kept Thea from her father? Would Thea be angry? Would Thea reject Lizzie in favour of the man who could give her so much more? And would it be right for Lizzie to stand in Thea's way if that was what Thea wanted?

She had to remain calm, Lizzie concluded. She could not go to pieces now. She'd been strong for eleven years, and if ever there was a time to be strong it was now. She couldn't move at the moment anyway. There were people blocking her way. All she could do was stand and watch Thea and Damon, wondering if she could have done something differently or better.

Shame. That was what she felt most. She should have found a way to tell them both the truth long before now.

And then, as if Lizzie and Thea were joined by some magical cord, Thea looked up and saw her.

Calling out, 'Mama! Mama!' at the top of her voice, she came running full pelt towards Lizzie.

'Mama!' Thea gasped when she reached Lizzie's side. 'You *must* come and meet my new friend, Damon Gavros! Okay—you stay there,' she said when Lizzie remained unresponsive. 'Save him a seat and I'll make sure he sits next to you. I've lined him up for a date with you later. I told him how beautiful you are—'

Racing away again, Thea retraced her steps and re-joined her friends in the orchestra.

Could a heart break and shatter into pieces? When Lizzie saw Damon's face she felt sure it could.

'Come with me,' Damon said when he reached her side.

He spoke quietly, but in a tone so hostile that everyone around them turned to stare.

'I can't—the concert's about to begin.' Lizzie glanced at the stage where Thea was sitting.

Thea was her anchor. She couldn't move.

'You can and you *will* come with me,' Damon assured her. 'The children don't play their pieces until after the speeches of welcome, and what I have to say to you won't take long.'

She couldn't make a scene—not here, of all places. Thea was sneaking glances at Lizzie to see how her matchmaking was working out. The last thing Lizzie wanted was to give Thea anything to worry about just before her concert began.

'Okay,' she agreed.

Smiling and waving at Thea, she indicated how long she'd be with five fingers held up.

Thea's smile was so broad and her eyes were so bright with hope that Lizzie knew she'd never felt so ashamed in her life as she walked away with Damon. There was disappointing your child, and then there was completely betraying her.

Damon ushered her ahead of him inside the school, where they would have some privacy. It was cool after the heat of the sun, and deserted. Their footsteps echoed on the tiled floor as he led the way into a classroom.

Closing the door, he leaned back against it, trapping them inside the empty room. 'When were you going to tell me?'

When Thea knew, of course.

She raised her chin to confront a man she barely recognised. Damon had pitched his voice low, but it was harsh with shock and anger. She stood about six feet away, with nothing to hang on to except her determination to try and do the right thing.

'I planned to tell you as soon as I had explained to Thea that you were back in our lives.' And then another horrible thought struck her. 'Have you told Thea?'

'Do you think I'm *mad*?' Damon's eyes flared with rage. 'How could you think I'd do something like that?'

'Because I don't know you—' That was true. She didn't know the man he had become. 'It's been a long time, Damon.'

'A *very* long time,' he agreed in a voice turned to ice.

Remembering Thea's happy face the moment she'd spotted Lizzie, waiting to take her seat, Lizzie knew she was overreacting in this instance, and that neither Damon nor Thea had made any connection between them until Thea had run up to Lizzie. Then Damon must have known.

'And in all that *very long time* you couldn't find the right moment to tell me that we had a child?'

He was incredulous. And furious. But she was armed too. 'It wasn't all about *you*, Damon.'

'Or you,' he fired back. 'Was a child so unimportant you just forgot to mention it?'

'Thea—not *a child*. And there is *nothing* more important to me than Thea.'

'How about giving me a chance to feel the same?' he suggested cuttingly.

Damon was incandescent with fury, but she hadn't expressed her feelings for almost eleven years. She hadn't had that luxury. She'd been too busy being a mother and keeping food on the table, a roof over their heads.

'I had a lot going on,' she said, battling to rein herself in. 'When I did try to contact you, your people blocked me, and I didn't have the resources to keep on trying to call. And even if I had...' She shrugged angrily. 'What would you have done?'

His jaw ground tensely. 'I wouldn't have been as insensitive as *you*.'

'Insensitive?' Lizzie clenched her fists. 'This from the man who turned his back on me after the court case, in spite having slept with me the night before? No doubt you'd washed your hands of everything to do with my family by that time. You'd got your victory, so everything else—including me—was done and dusted.'

'I moved on—as you did,' Damon countered coldly.

'I moved on because I had to. I didn't have a home to go to. You walked away without a backward glance.' Her shoulders lifted tensely. 'You didn't care what happened to me after the court case.'

'You weren't my responsibility,' Damon said coldly, and with a good deal of truth.

'Correct,' Lizzie agreed. 'But you can be quick to help those you want to, can't you Damon? You just couldn't see beyond bedding me, and you certainly didn't *care* about me, did you? So don't you dare come back now and start accusing me of handling things badly. We both made mistakes—'

'You can't turn this around on me.'

'Why not?' Lizzie challenged. '*You* walked away.'

'There was nothing to walk away *from*.'

With a shake of her head, she laughed angrily. 'Exactly. All I am to you—all I ever was—is a one-night stand.'

'And you had so much going on in your life that letting me know you were expecting my child came well down the list.'

'You just don't get it, do you?' Lizzie exclaimed. 'I didn't have your resources. I was thrown out of my childhood home with just the clothes I stood up in. I didn't have any money. I certainly didn't have a phone. I didn't know where my next meal was coming from, let alone whether I could manage to put a roof over my head. And at that stage, Damon, you were the *last* person I'd have thought of calling. Why would I, when you'd made no attempt to find me?

'I had no one to rely on but myself—and don't think for one moment that I'm complaining, because it was a good thing. Being alone taught me self-reliance and helped me to be a better mother for Thea. It made me strong and determined, and I learned that if I took one step at a time I could survive—I could put a roof over my head and I could care for my baby. Those were the only things that mattered to me—not you, nor me. Beyond keeping healthy for Thea's sake, the only thing I cared about—still care about and always will care about—is Thea.'

'You should have come to me,' he ground out.

'Should I?' she demanded. 'If I could have found you, do you mean? After I'd repeatedly contacted your people and been turned away I made one attempt to appeal to my stepmother, one woman to another. I told her I was pregnant and begged her to help me find you. She laughed in my face and told me never to return. She couldn't have a slut damaging her reputation, she said. Yes, it was a slap in the face,' Lizzie agreed, 'but it pulled me together fast and I managed very well without her—and without you too. It didn't take me long to learn that I was better on my own.'

'You didn't give me the chance,' Damon said with a shake of his head. 'You didn't give me the chance to know my child. And, yes, I was away for a lot of the time, but since I came back I've taken you out twice, and yet you never hinted that we had a daughter together. Do you have an explanation for that?'

'Yes, I do. Thea had to know first. I was protecting *her*. And if you can't see that then you're not fit to call yourself her father. *That's* the difference between you and me,' she added. 'You have all the power and money in the world, and I have nothing, but when it comes to Thea you won't get past me.'

'I wouldn't be so sure. I have rights,' he said.

'You have *no* rights,' Lizzie argued, feeling calmer.

'*I*… I have no rights?'

Damon almost laughed—as well he might. A man who could command anything that money could buy, would find it difficult, if not impossible, to conceive that there was something on this earth he couldn't have.

Lizzie felt as if ice had invaded her veins, but nothing would stop her when she was in defence of her child, and Damon had to hear this. 'You have no rights because there's no father listed on Thea's birth certificate.'

'A DNA test would soon establish my rights as Thea's father,' he said confidently.

'*If* I allowed such a test to take place.' Lizzie lifted her chin. 'The fact that your name doesn't appear on Thea's birth certificate means that you have no legal rights over Thea unless I allow you to.'

'I'll fight you every way I can,' Damon threatened, frowning.

'Again?' Lizzie said quietly. 'Before you deploy your legal team, you should know this. Thea doesn't want to know her father. She never has. She asked me to stop talking about him because we were all right as we were, and she didn't want some mystery man entering her life.'

'She might change her mind if she knew it was me.'

Damon's voice was so cold it chilled her.

A burst of applause drew their attention to the window. The conductor was mounting the stage.

'I have to go.' She turned for the door. Damon remained where he was. She hesitated with her hand on the door handle. Squeezing her eyes tightly shut, she drew in a breath and then turned back to face him. 'You should hear her play. You'll regret it if you don't.'

She walked out of the room and didn't stop until she was outside the school. She felt as if she were suffocating, and gulped in air. There was no one behind her…no sound…no footsteps…no Damon.

He was incapable of feeling anything—numb, existing on autopilot. He was breathing, maybe. He stood in the silence of an empty room until the first swell of music from the youth orchestra prompted him to act.

Lizzie was easy to spot, with her shining red hair in a sea of ebony locks. There was only one empty seat left in the entire audience and that was next to her. He could have stood at the back, or at the side, but that might have looked odd to Thea.

Lizzie didn't acknowledge him as he sat down. He didn't acknowledge her. They might have been two strangers. Two strangers with a daughter between them.

He had a daughter.

He kept on repeating the phrase over and over in his head, as if it would finally make some sense to him.

The young musical sensation Thea Floros was his daughter… Floros was Lizzie's mother's maiden name.

The pieces clicked into place one after the other

as he sat immobile in a state of shock. Another part of his brain was agitatedly wondering how to make up for eleven years. He had a child, and that changed everything.

The little violinist he'd got on with so well with was his daughter. And Thea was her name. He had a daughter named Thea...

Repeating this was both surprising and wonderful, and he kept on repeating it as the orchestra played.

'Damon?'

He heard Lizzie murmur something to him, but he couldn't answer. He didn't want to answer her. He didn't want to speak to her. He wasn't ready to share the way he felt right now with anyone—especially Lizzie. He couldn't have put his thoughts into words, anyway, and not just because the concert had started and even a cough would be inappropriate. They couldn't discuss something as monumental as this in public.

Where could they discuss it?

There was no approved course of action. All his experience had left him completely unprepared for this. He was encased in ice, preserved and separate, untouchable, unreachable—as Lizzie had complained he was all those years ago.

He registered without emotion that this strange state of non-feeling stillness must be the calm before the storm. When he blew he would take everything with him.

And then Thea stood up.

At first he stared at her, as if she were an automaton in a museum, safe behind glass, and he was a visitor showing a passing interest in one of the exhibits. If he felt anything it was curiosity—that he could look at his daughter and not know what to feel.

But then she lifted her bow and started to play.

CHAPTER NINE

MUSIC COULD TOUCH HIM. It always had been able to touch him. Thanks to his father's passion, music had always played a huge part in his home-life when he'd been growing up. Music could unlock him, and now Thea had freed emotions inside him that he hadn't even known were there.

They must have been locked away for years as he drove forward with the business, allowing nothing to distract him. At the time he'd thought emotion a selfish indulgence and it had become a habit, he supposed. His focus had been all on working as hard as he could so his father could retire. It was only now, as Thea wove magic with her violin, that he realised how empty his life had become.

His daughter was filling it—filling him—with emotion, until it threatened to overflow. The melody she was playing so skilfully was uncomplicated, but it tugged at his heart and forced a response from him. Eleven years he'd missed of this child's life. Eleven years. Feeling her kick in the womb, seeing her born and holding her in his arms for the first time, celebrating her first birthday and the elation of watching as she took her first steps—all gone. Hearing her first words and encouraging her to stride out bravely on her first day at school—

'Damon? *Damon....?*'

Someone was shaking his shoulder, he realised, coming to fast. Feeling tears on his cheeks, he swiped them away.

His aide dipped down to speak to him. 'I'm sorry to break in on your private time,' the man whispered, 'but we have an emergency at one of the plants—a fire. It's contained now, but we could do with your steer on to how to handle the aftermath.'

'I'm with you,' he said, getting up. His workers were another family to him, and almost as close as his own. Whatever they needed, he was there.

Thea was family. Thea was his family.

His stare met Thea's as he rose from his seat. It was a magical split-second. Fate had dictated that she finish her solo just as he stood. Everyone was standing to applaud. He had hoped she wouldn't notice him leaving. He might have known she would know immediately. She was his daughter, after all.

She smiled at him—a smile that lit his world. It was innocent and happy and he smiled back, held his daughter's open, trusting gaze, while the woman at his side—Lizzie—tugged at his arm repeatedly.

He pulled away sharply. Her hand was an unwanted intrusion on his naked skin. Raising his hands to applaud Thea, he ignored his aide's edginess and obvious desire to go. He could spare these few seconds to let Thea understand and see how deeply he had appreciated her performance.

For each second he held eye contact with Thea he could feel Lizzie's distress. Her tugs were becoming more insistent, and her voice, though it seemed to come from a long way away, was obviously distraught. But he couldn't be distracted. His attention was centred on his daughter—as if in these few seconds he was making up for eleven years of separation.

'Damon—'

'I'm coming,' he snapped at his aide.

With one last long look at Thea, he moved into the aisle and strode away.

Lizzie sat in her seat motionless long after the other audience members had left. People moved past her. She barely registered them. She felt cloaked in doom, and it was a doom of her own making. Of all the ways for Damon to find about Thea, this had to be the worst. How must it have felt for him to be sitting next to his daughter's mother, only to discover that the woman he had made love to was apparently as untrustworthy as her scumbag father?

She had felt Damon quite literally shrink away from her. And she'd seen the look he'd given Thea. It had been the leader of the wolf pack acknowledging his cub. If the thought of a blood relationship between Damon and Thea hadn't struck anyone else yet, it soon would. The ease between them, coupled with their incredible likeness, signalled their bond like a flashing beacon.

Thea was a bright child. How long would it take *her* to work it out?

Having never heard Thea express the need for a father, Lizzie began to wonder if that had been to save her feelings. They had been a team of two for ever, and now they were three—though not a team, and without any explanation from Lizzie.

She found herself flinching when Thea came running down the aisle, swinging her violin case as if she didn't have a care in the world.

And why should she?

But everything was about to change for Thea. Remembering how that had felt for herself when she was eighteen—almost twice Thea's age, with twice Thea's experience of life—Lizzie shrank a little more inside.

'Mama!' Thea exclaimed. 'Did you enjoy the concert?' Thea was hopping from foot to foot, still fired up on adrenalin, when she reached Lizzie's side. 'Did you notice that note I got wrong?'

'I only noticed that you played beautifully,' Lizzie said honestly, on a throat so tight she could hardly breathe.

'I played for *you*,' Thea announced, throwing her arms around her mother to hug her tight.

This was the wake-up call she needed, Lizzie realised. She *wasn't* a useless mother. She was just a mother and she'd always done her best. She was a hostage for life, and she welcomed that knowledge. She'd no doubt get things wrong again in the future, but she'd always strive to put them right. She would never stop trying when it came to Thea.

'I can't wait to hear you play again,' she said warmly when a few of Thea's friends gathered round. 'I think you're amazing—all of you.'

Lizzie's heart melted when Thea turned a beaming smile on her friends, as if to say, *This is my mother and she really gets us.*

'Love you, darling!' Lizzie called out as Thea raced away with her friends.

Glancing across the playing fields, Lizzie could see Thea and her group of friends gathering up a feast from the buffet, to carry off and eat beneath the shade of the olive trees. Sensing Lizzie was still staring at her, Thea turned and gestured vigorously that Lizzie must join them.

Lizzie drew a deep breath and told herself firmly that whatever happened next she could deal with it. She had dealt with things for eleven years now, and would continue to do so. She would do anything to protect Thea.

And Damon? What about him?

She'd lost him before she'd had chance to know him. He could never be part of her life now—though he would surely be part of Thea's. That would be up to Thea, Lizzie determined as she hurried across the parched playing field to join the children.

'There he goes!' Thea yelled, pointing to the sky as Lizzie approached.

Shading her eyes, Lizzie stared up as the rhythmical thwack of a helicopter's rotor blades passed overhead. Damon would be flying off to wherever he was needed most, she guessed.

Guilt flooded her again. She'd worked so hard to get things right for Thea, and now she'd fallen at this, the last hurdle. She might never get the chance to speak to Damon again except through lawyers, and she had always planned to bring Thea and Damon together carefully, sensitively—anywhere *but* in a courtroom.

She shuddered at the thought. There was no excuse, although her reasons for not telling Damon sooner were complex and mostly rooted in the past. Believing he'd deserted her too, so soon after her father's rejection, she'd vowed never to love again, never to risk her heart again—and she had kept that vow until Thea was born, when she had discovered a love so deep it had almost drowned her.

Her father's rejection, coming at such a vulnerable and hormonal time in Lizzie's life, had left her with an overwhelming desire to protect Thea from that same pain.

Looking back, she saw that the world her father had aspired to was shallow, and based on what people had in the bank rather than what they were really worth, and that in turn had left her with a lifelong suspicion of wealth. She knew deep down that Damon was a different kind of rich, and that he'd not only worked hard for everything he'd got but had done good with that money. But the glamorous world he inhabited still troubled her. She would never belong in a world like that—though in time Thea might, Lizzie allowed.

'Okay...' Thea looked up expectantly at her mother.

'Okay, what?' Lizzie asked lightly, pinning a smile to her face.

'Do. You. Like. Him?' Thea asked, testing her facial muscles to their limit. 'Damon Gavros,' she explained impatiently. 'I saw him sitting next to you. We *all* did,' Thea added, grinning as she gazed around at her friends.

So now she had an audience. Lizzie's stomach sank. She shrugged and smiled through it. 'Of course I like him. What's not to like?'

'Well, that's good,' Thea said. 'Because he's on his way over—'

'What?' Lizzie's world tilted as she swung around in panic.

Damon was not supposed to be here. He'd just flown away in his helicopter.

'We're all thrilled you like him,' Thea said, her voice penetrating Lizzie's fog of incomprehension, 'because we need ice cream and we're hoping he'll buy some.'

If only life were that simple, Lizzie thought. She almost laughed. Impending hysteria, she guessed. It took a child to point out the obvious. There was ice cream, and there was a man with enough money to buy each of them a serving. Damon was no more complex or disturbing than that as far as Thea was concerned.

And long may it remain that way, Lizzie thought.

'Why don't you stay here with your friends while I go and see what he says to your suggestion?' she offered.

'Not *he*—Damon,' Thea insisted. 'You have to use his name if you stand a hope of getting close to him.'

'Right…' Lizzie pressed her lips together in a thin smile.

She had no chance of getting close to Damon, but now wasn't the time to disillusion Thea. There was no more time to waste. She had to head him off before he reached them and Thea sensed that something was wrong.

'Damon—Damon Gavros!' Thea called after her. 'He has the same name as this island. You can't forget it.'

She would *never* forget it, since it was gouged on her heart, Lizzie thought as she called back to Thea, 'Back soon. Sit tight and I'll see what I can do.'

'Not too soon!' Thea yelled after her. 'We've got stuff to do…so you've got the whole evening with *Damon*. See you tomorrow!'

As the children's giggles rose behind her Lizzie knew she had to make things right before they got a lot worse. She had to reach a compromise with Damon if they weren't going to end up fighting each other through every court in the land. Though how she was supposed to fight Damon Gavros and his legal team, she had no idea.

Not yet, Lizzie thought, firming her jaw, but when it came to Thea she'd fight to the death.

He was feeling icy calm as he strode across the field towards Lizzie. Business could do that for him. He could always see the way ahead where his work was concerned. It cleared his head when other areas of his life were complicated. He had given precise instructions to his aide so the fallout after the fire would be dealt with. Everyone would receive the care and compensation they deserved. He wouldn't stint. He never did where family was concerned.

And now for Lizzie, who was coming to meet him, diverting him away from the group of children— which was just as well. When they were a few feet apart he jerked his head to suggest she follow him. He noticed Thea was watching, and smiled for her benefit.

The multinational conglomerate he controlled with such ease was nothing compared to the complexities of human relationships, he decided. *This* was the minefield, right here. He felt no animosity towards Lizzie. He felt nothing. But his mind was made up. The direction they would take from here was clear. Lizzie might have procrastinated for eleven years, but making fast decisions based on the evidence in front of him had always been his forte.

He led the way to his helicopter and noticed the moment when realisation struck Lizzie. Damon had two helicopters. In fact he had a fleet of helicopters. He never knew when he or one of his executives would need to move fast. He had never needed to move faster than he did now.

He opened the passenger door and made sure Lizzie was settled before helping her to fasten her harness and explaining how her headphones worked. There was no tension or anger in his voice. There was nothing. Lizzie's face paled, as if she found his manner more chilling than if he'd raged at her.

The short flight brought them above his beach house. It was here that the future would be spelled out.

A kaleidoscope of images flashed through Lizzie's panicked mind as the helicopter hovered over Damon's spectacular beach house—or mansion, as Lizzie thought of it. The contrast of the simple home she'd made for Thea with this, and with all Damon's other homes across the world, was painfully stark.

She could get a sense of perspective through the clear floor of the helicopter beneath her feet... The carefully cultivated gardens, the Olympic-size swimming pool and the tennis courts beyond. There was even a putting green. Ivory sand fringed the bright blue ocean in front of the house, and she could see Damon's cutting-edge powerboat rolling gently on the lazy waves.

Compare that to a grimy London street and a front door that opened on to someone else's hallway and it was no wonder her heart was beating in double time.

And it wasn't just Damon's possessions or his way of life that she found so threatening, but his superkeen intelligence and innate skill. Damon might say he'd had advantages, and he had, but he'd taken them, and transformed his father's business into a stratospheric success. Some people took a bus to work, while others—like Damon—handled a helicopter with the same ease as a compact car, she mused as the sleek craft settled seamlessly on its skids.

What would Damon make of their daughter's obsession with thrift shops? Lizzie wondered as Damon came around to help her out. Would he understand that Thea needed to express her quirky side with things she couldn't find on the High Street? Or would he think that Lizzie's lack of financial resources had condemned Thea to wearing second-hand clothes? Would he understand *anything* about Thea?

Was it wrong and selfish of Lizzie to think, *Thea is my baby*? Was it wrong to look down at Damon's capable hands as he freed her harness and refuse to acknowledge that this man had played an equal part in the creation of their child?

Thea is the child I carried in my belly, and then on my hip, and always, always in my heart, Lizzie thought as Damon walked ahead of her.

But he could offer Thea so much more than she could. Thea had to confine her violin practice to one hour a day in London when she was at home, or they would have to find somewhere else to live. That was what the owners of the house had told Lizzie. How many music studios could Thea have in a house like this?

Sparkling white granite chippings crunched beneath their feet as they walked up the elegant path towards the front door. Everywhere she looked was something amazing…the vast planting arrangements at each side of the door, the banks of flowers below the windows, all immaculately groomed.

Damon could easily afford to buy any priceless violin Thea set her heart on, Lizzie thought as he in-

serted a code into the panel at the side of the door
and it swung open. *She* had to work three jobs just to
pay for the extra sheet music Thea needed for school.

By the time the door opened she had worked herself up into a real state. Damon had all the power in
the world. She had none. He had a legal team at his
beck and call. She didn't even have enough money
to call a lawyer in England from Greece.

Was she about to lose Thea?

No! Lizzie thought fiercely. Not while she had
breath in her body.

She walked into the vaulted hallway and stared
around numbly. Whatever she had expected Damon's
new house to be like, this was so much *more*. The
space, the light, the air, the simple luxury surrounding her... It was all extremely tasteful, with décor in a
palette of soft neutral shades. And it was empty—as if
waiting for someone to move in and imbue it with life.

This was not the way he had imagined it would be
when he brought Lizzie into his new home for the
first time. They had only looked at it from the beach
before, because—ironically—they'd had to get back
for Thea's concert. Fresh from making love to Lizzie,
he'd had the crazy notion of sweeping her into his
arms and carrying her across the threshold. And then
they'd make love on every surface in the house.

Not this time.

He led the way into a lavishly equipped but as
yet unoccupied study. The room was spectacular. A
wall of glass faced the electric blue bay, and the desk

was a long, plain piece of wood, its only ornament a computer. The surface of the desk was as smooth as glass. He'd planned, prepped and planed it himself, finishing it with beeswax.

As Lizzie ran her fingertips over the surface he remembered the pleasure he'd had making it, the simple joy of working with his hands. Creating things like the desk allowed him to escape the rattle of business for a while and just *be*. Simplicity in all things always gave him pleasure. Honesty did the same.

He drew a breath and turned to face Lizzie.

'Damon, I—'

He silenced her with a raised hand. 'Please. Sit down.'

'I'd rather stand, if you don't mind.'

The tension in Lizzie's voice was like a taut band on the point of snapping. He felt no pity. Beyond knowing that if she broke down it would delay things and get them nowhere, he felt no empathy at all. He positioned himself with his back to the window while Lizzie remained by the door. He saw a flicker of fear in her eyes, but then it was gone. She was determined to stand up to him. But he held all the cards and she held none—they both knew that.

Although he hadn't forgotten Lizzie's determination to refuse him equal rights, and the fact that he wasn't even mentioned on Thea's birth certificate...

On reflection, it seemed that perhaps Lizzie held the trump card.

Her arms were ramrod-straight against her sides, her fists clenched so tight her knuckles were like polished ivory. The blood had drained from her cheeks and her eyes were huge in the ashen wasteland of her face. He had experienced emotion briefly, when Thea had played the violin, but whatever his daughter had unlocked was gone now. It was for Thea alone. He dealt with all problems the same way—by being incisive and emotion-free—and he would do that now.

'You don't know her,' Lizzie told him quietly, as if anticipating what he might say. 'Thea doesn't know you. You can't just walk into her life and claim her, Damon.'

'You don't know *what* I can do.'

Her lips had turned white. She knew the power he wielded.

Her brow pleated. 'Are you trying to intimidate me?'

'Never,' he stated factually. 'I am simply trying to reclaim what's mine.'

'And what then?' she asked him tensely.

'That's what I have to find out. I have to find a solution.'

'*We* have to find a solution,' Lizzie argued quietly.

'You've lost your chance,' he said frankly. 'It's my turn now. I think you should sit down. We have to put our personal differences aside and consider what's best for Thea.'

'Thea is all I ever think about,' Lizzie assured him, with a blaze of passion in her eyes.

'I haven't been given that chance,' he pointed out with supreme restraint.

The disappointment he felt in Lizzie was acute.

She was as shallow as the rest of them. Self-interest ruled her. She might never have told him that they had a daughter together if he hadn't walked into that restaurant in London. She would have kept Thea to herself.

Pain stabbed him when he thought about the years that had been lost. He had to turn away for a few moments and pour them both a glass of iced water to give him something else to focus on while his rage subsided.

'Why aren't you angry?' Lizzie demanded.

He almost laughed.

'Are you incapable of feelings?'

'Declara!'

He'd spilled the water on his desk. *Incapable of feelings?* This entire situation had rocked the foundations of his life.

Snatching up a cloth, he mopped up the spill before turning to face her. 'Perhaps *you* can afford to be emotional, but I can't. How would it look in business if I railed at my competitors and made every decision on a wave of passion?'

'This isn't a *business* decision,' she fired back. 'This is our daughter. *Thea.*'

'I'm glad you've finally remembered,' he countered with scorn.

'So this is just another exercise in winning for you?' Lizzie suggested.

'Far from it.'

She had no idea of the turmoil inside him. He'd only ever known happy, uncomplicated love—love without boundaries, the type of love that a parent gave to a child, the style of unconditional love that his parents had given to him. It was love without demands, love that would sacrifice everything, and he hadn't been given the chance to experience that same love with Thea.

The love he felt for Thea already was incalculable. It was as if eleven years had been compacted into a single day of knowing and loving his child. His head was reeling with love. Eleven years of Thea's existence had been lost, never to be reclaimed. From the night of her conception to the night before her birth, when she'd been nothing more than a tiny light waiting to take a tilt at life, and on to this moment, here in his study, where he was talking about Thea to her mother.

All of those precious moments were lost. Everything that had been Thea before now had gone, never to be reclaimed.

CHAPTER TEN

HIS LOST TIME with Thea had lodged in his heart, where it was lashing around, demanding an explanation. Lizzie thought that because he was acting so contained he felt nothing, when for the first time in his life he didn't know if he could trust himself to handle this meeting as well as he must. He only knew that for Thea's sake he had to.

In order to bring himself to talk to Lizzie at all, he had listed the *good* things she had done. Thea had turned out well. Raising her as a single mother with no family couldn't have been easy for Lizzie. Eleven years ago she had been just eighteen and pregnant, with no home, no money, no family—no one at all to rely on but herself. She hadn't just *cared* for Thea, she loved Thea without boundaries, in the same way that he'd been loved as a child, and Lizzie had raised Thea without the good fortune his parents had enjoyed.

He couldn't claim any credit for Thea beyond her existence. She was all Lizzie's work. That was why he'd found Lizzie washing pots in London. It all made sense now. She'd kept nothing for herself and had put all her dreams on indefinite hold for Thea.

But Thea was *his* daughter too, and he had been denied every moment of her existence—even the knowledge of it—up to now. So, although he could rationalise the situation and give Lizzie some credit, things could not go on as they were.

'I won't let you take her, Damon.'

He stared at Lizzie. He'd seen flashes of her vulnerability, but it would be a mistake to think her vulnerable now. His mother had always told him that there was no stronger opponent a man could face than a mother fighting for her child.

'No court would allow any man to walk into a child's life and take her from the mother who has loved her from the instant she first felt her stir in the womb—who has loved her unreservedly ever since—unless that man could prove both that he was the father of the child and that the mother was unfit to care for her. And no one—not even you—can prove a lie, Damon.'

'I'm not just any man,' he argued tensely. 'I'm a father. *Thea's* father.'

'I will fight you every step of the way,' she warned him. 'I'll fight your money, your power, and your legal team too. Do you *really* think you can defeat a mother in defence of her child? Even *you* don't have the weapons for that, Damon.'

His feelings were rising. He felt fury that she would deny him Thea even now—and yet he knew acceptance, however reluctant, that his own mother would have said the same.

He wasn't as callous as Lizzie thought him. She had been in his thoughts too. She'd never left them, really. In the desert, when he'd been working with his team, she had intruded on his thoughts at night, and in the day he'd kept her in mind to ease some of the horrors he'd seen. But she'd kept the most important thing on earth from him, and he could never forgive her for that.

She had cheated him out of Thea, as her father had cheated his father. How could he ever trust her again after that?

'You'll have to—' He'd been about to say, *consult a lawyer*, when Lizzie leapt ahead of him—but in the wrong direction.

'I don't have to do anything you tell me to,' she assured him. 'It's up to you to launch your case—try to destroy me as you destroyed my father.'

'Lizzie…' he modulated his tone. 'We've been over this ground several times. We both know that what happened in court that day was for the best.'

'What *I* know is that my father was weak and you were strong. Is that what you plan to do now? Crush me?'

Grinding his jaw, he refused to be drawn, but Lizzie had the bit between her teeth.

'Get this straight,' she blazed at him. 'Thea stays with *me*. We choose a time to tell her that you're her father, and we do that together. Above all we try to be civilised about this.'

'And then Thea makes her choice,' he said mildly, employing all the reason he used in business. 'Thea isn't a baby. She's a highly intelligent girl with a mind of her own. There isn't a judge alive who wouldn't want to hear what she has to say.'

Lizzie's heart lurched. Closing her eyes briefly, she reeled through a new scene in court. Penniless mother. Billionaire father. What would the judge make of that?

It was a matter of trust, she concluded. It boiled down to her belief in the strength of the love that she and Thea shared. It was just the thought of that love being put to the test in front of strangers that made her feel terrible for Thea. Why should a ten-year-old child have to go through that? This was never what she'd wanted.

'We'll see,' was all she could reply.

When it came down to it, love was all about trust, Lizzie reflected. Yes, love could be hurt and doubt, but it was also hope. She'd lost all hope of love with Damon, but Thea's future was still untarnished— and it would remain that way if Lizzie had anything to do with it.

'Tell me one thing,' she said. 'Did you never once feel guilty for walking away after casually destroying my life?'

'You left with your friends, as I remember it.'

And her life *had* badly needed shaking up. She accepted that.

'What happened to those friends?' Damon probed.

'When the money ran out, so did they,' she admitted frankly. 'Fair-weather friends, as you yourself called them. I made a clean start. I was lucky enough to make more friends—real friends—who couldn't have cared less if I could afford to wear this label or that, or if my father gave the most lavish parties. Though in fairness to those old friends,' she admitted, 'their parents wouldn't allow them to see me. First there was the shame of my father's imprisonment, and then the fear that I might want a loan to see me through, and finally, to cap it all, I was pregnant, with no sign of a husband or partner.'

'So, not really your friends at all, then?' Damon said.

'No,' Lizzie agreed. 'I know the difference now. Being pregnant with Thea gave me a very clear focus on life. Motherhood changed me for good. I grew up overnight. I had to, to make a go of things for Thea. I even found that I wasn't so stupid after all.' She shrugged wryly. 'Being a mother was actually something I was good at.'

He couldn't deny that. 'But you should have contacted me.'

'I did! I told you that I was blocked by your people.'

'You should have kept trying until you reached me. I would have helped you if I'd known. I would have definitely wanted to be part of Thea's life.'

'*Would* you? Can you be so sure of how you would have reacted back then? You were a lot younger too, Damon, and you've had a long way to travel to reach this point. Domesticity would have hindered your progress. It might even have stopped you setting out.'

'Domesticity?' he queried with a frown.

'Just a figure of speech,' Lizzie said coolly. 'Perhaps it's all worked out for the best. One day I might show you the stack of unopened letters I sent to your office. They were all marked "Returned to sender". I wrote to you as soon as I was settled,' she explained, in answer to his unspoken question. 'I *did* think about you and the part you should be playing in our lives. And not just because of your money, Damon. I was never interested in that.'

'What part are you talking about, then? A full part?'

'That would have had to be decided then—just as it has to be decided now. I can only tell you that your personnel team deserves a collective medal for protecting your privacy.'

He could believe that. He was never readily available to anyone outside his immediate family. Those who didn't have him on speed dial—which was most of the world—had to jump through many hoops before they could even reach the assistant to his assistant PA. Reaching his PA was next to impossible.

'I *did* want you to know about Thea,' Lizzie insisted quietly, 'but I didn't want anything else from you—not in a material sense.'

She turned away from him and gazed off into the middle distance. He guessed she was reliving all the exultation, fear and hope of an expectant mother. She'd had no one to share those moments with…no family, no parents, no one at all. And then, when Thea had arrived, she must have been like a ray of sunshine, bringing happiness into every life she touched, just as she'd touched his already.

'Where *were* you?' Lizzie demanded angrily, perhaps taking his smile as he thought about Thea for scorn. 'Where were you when I was being examined by the midwife and not knowing what to expect? Where were you when they were taking scans of Thea and I was scared half to death, thinking they might find something wrong with her because I couldn't always afford the best food or to eat healthily? Where you were you when I was in labour and frightened? Where were you when your daughter was born? Where were you when they took blood from her heel and she cried with pain? *Where were you when I needed you?*'

As Lizzie's voice tightened into a wordless scream he didn't think about the past, the present or the future. He didn't think about the rights and wrongs of the situation at all. He just grabbed her close and held her tightly to him as tears streamed down her face. And then he kissed her, and kept on kissing her, while she shuddered and then remembered to fight him—punching and shouting as she vented her frustration, until her passion veered onto a different track and she clung to him like a drowning man to a raft.

'Hey, stop…stop…' he insisted, kissing her face, her eyes, her lips, her brow. 'Calm down, Lizzie—'

'Calm down?' she demanded, rallying enough to pull back. 'Can't you see what I stand to lose, you stupid man? *Everything!*'

Beautiful, tempestuous Lizzie. *This* was the woman who had bewitched him eleven years ago. He'd calmed her then, but could he calm her now? Even *he* didn't know. He'd never seen a human being so distraught.

Sweeping her into his arms, he carried her into one of the bedrooms and kept on kissing her as he shouldered the door closed behind them. He kissed her as he carried her to the bed, and she made no attempt to move away when he put her down. She made no attempt to move at all beyond covering her eyes with her forearm as he kicked off his shoes.

Stretching out his length against her, he drew her into his arms with the intention of soothing her—but Lizzie was way ahead of him. Fingers flying over the buttons down the front of her dress, she whipped it over her head. When he attempted to take it from her she defended the cheap sundress like a lioness. Folding the soft yellow material neatly, she leaned across the bed to place it on a chair.

'No, Lizzie…no.'

He'd planned to take things slowly, but the moment he turned to face her she sprang into his arms and, lacing her fingers through his hair, wrapped her legs around him, kissing him as if they were facing the end of the world.

He considered himself a just man, but he wasn't a saint, and primal need soon overcame his finer feelings. Doubt, rage and resentment forgotten, he ripped off his clothes, only knowing that he'd missed her. *Theos!* How much!

* * *

Her hunger to blank everything out was all Lizzie could think about—that and claiming her mate, maybe for the last time. There was no chance for foreplay, or for teasing advances. Delaying tactics of any type were barred. She needed oblivion *now*.

She exclaimed in triumph as Damon threw her on her back. Planting his fists either side of her head, he loomed over her—big, powerful, majestic and ultra-efficient when it came to mind-blanking.

Drawing her knees back, she locked her legs around his waist. She knew exactly what she was inviting, and she exulted in the shock of his possession as Damon plunged deep. She lost control immediately. She didn't spare a thought for whether she should or not. There was no finesse, no manners at all.

Shrieking and bucking, she grabbed at him, driving him on with her fingers pressed mercilessly into the steel of his buttocks. She was determined to catch every last throb of pleasure, and when sensation robbed her of thought she exclaimed gratefully and noisily in time to each crashing wave.

'More!' she gasped as she dragged in some much-needed air.

She was laughing with excitement as Damon dragged her to the edge of the bed. Arranging her to his liking, with her hips balanced precariously on the edge, he pressed her legs back and stood between them.

'You like it deep? You like it firm?' he suggested, with the faintest of smiles on his mouth.

'What do *you* think?' she challenged.

Lifting her legs onto his shoulders, he rewarded her with a fierce, fast rhythm that had her plunging over the edge almost at once.

'Greedy,' he growled, sounding pleased.

Bringing her into his arms, he carried her across the room to the wall of windows. 'Is *this* what you want?' he said as he pushed her naked body against the glass. 'Now the whole world can see the butterflies you've got tattooed on your backside.'

Dipping at the knees, he thrust deep and relentlessly, until she came apart in his arms, wailing and shrieking.

When she gasped, 'Too good…' he demanded to know if she had any more tattoos that required his attention.

'Why don't you take a look?' she suggested.

She'd been starved for too long, Lizzie realised, as Damon continued to move deep inside her and she continued to bask in oblivion, where sensation ruled—*or was that to hide?*—

Again? Really? Was *again* even possible?

It was, she discovered, wailing as she fell.

This time it was so intense, and lasted so long, she might even have lost consciousness for a few moments. When she came round it was to find Damon still moving steadily and deeply, his big, slightly roughened hands locked firmly as he kept her in position for each firm thrust.

'Don't do anything,' he commanded in a low, husky tone. 'Don't move at all. Relax every muscle and let me do all the work.'

She did as he asked and was rewarded with plea-sure. Clearly seeing it in her eyes, Damon smiled fiercely against her mouth, and as he kissed her he rotated his hips, keeping them tightly locked together, and she fell again.

'What about you?' she asked when she was finally able to speak.

Pulling out completely, Damon thrust deeply again, with a groan of satisfaction, and a few firm, fast strokes later he brought them both over the edge.

'Bed?' Lizzie suggested as he cupped her face in his hands.

'Lightweight,' Damon whispered against her mouth.

'You're insatiable.'

'And you seem pleased about that,' he commented.

'I am,' she admitted.

'You're the same,' he insisted. 'You just don't know it yet.'

'Then why don't you prove it to me?'

Swinging her into his arms, he carried her across the room and into his bathroom, which was the most opulent haven of luxury she'd ever seen. Black mar-ble covered the walls and floor, and there was elegant furniture. High-end products in industrial-sized crys-tal jars were just begging to be used. And there were mirrors everywhere.

The sight of herself in Damon's arms, both of them naked and intimately entwined, was the most arous-ing thing that Lizzie had ever seen.

'That insatiable thing…' Damon murmured as he steadied her on the warm marble floor.

'What about it?' Lifting her chin, she blazed a challenge into his eyes.

'It's time I proved it to you…'

CHAPTER ELEVEN

THIS WAS NOT like Lizzie's shower in London. No chance of a lukewarm dribble trickling out of a rusty showerhead. Damon's shower was a powerful blast of water at the perfect temperature, and it was instantly warm.

'Billionaire's perks?' Lizzie suggested as she turned her face towards the refreshing stream.

Taking the exclusive shower gel out of her hands, Damon washed her all over with long and increasingly intimate strokes. And then he trained the showerhead where she was most sensitive, skilfully massaging her with tiny, tantalising blunt-edged needles that took her arousal to new heights.

'Hands flat against the wall,' he instructed.

How could her body be so sensitive? The warm water had made her nerve-endings super-responsive, Lizzie supposed as Damon trained the water over her back and her buttocks.

Resting her head against the wall, she groaned with pleasure as he nudged her legs apart to direct the pounding water so skilfully she found yet another way to lose control. He caught her as her legs buckled beneath her, but even that wasn't enough for him. Resting her leg high on his thigh, he thrust into her, working steadily to bring her to the edge again.

'I can't...' she protested, shaking her head, certain this was true.

'Yes, you can,' he insisted softly—and he proved it beyond doubt.

After the shower he swaddled her in warm, fluffy towels and carried her back to bed. 'Sleep now,' he said.

'Sleep?' she complained softly, staring into his eyes.

'I have work to do,' Damon told her, pulling away.

And then, just like eleven years before, he was gone.

How had she ever managed to sleep? Lizzie wondered as she woke to find sunlight blazing into the room. *Damon's bedroom.* She turned over in bed. The other side was empty. The pillow was smooth. She'd slept through the night. But where was Damon?

As the events of the previous night came flooding back she sat up and realised that she'd had her first untroubled night's sleep without nightmares in ages. There had been no ghoulish return to a hushed courtroom full of haunted faces. She must have been totally exhausted to sleep like that. Having glutted herself on Damon, that was hardly a surprise. But now she sat up to listen she thought the house was empty.

She was just a temporary visitor who had outstayed

her welcome, Lizzie thought, feeling awkward as she swung herself out of the bed. They were supposed to be telling Thea today—that was what they'd decided in the dark hours of the night. Had Damon gone on ahead of her?

No! Thea must hear it from her mother, Lizzie thought as she rushed to take a shower.

As she stood beneath the water that had felt so soothing only hours before her mind filled with terrifying images. They included Damon taking Thea away on his powerboat, or in his helicopter, or his jet—how would she ever find them again when he had homes all over the world? She'd made a very poor job of finding Damon over the past eleven years, so he would easily stay ahead of her now.

Grabbing a towel, she closed her eyes and accepted that her fears had no base in reality. All she had to do was get herself back to the restaurant somehow, so she could change her clothes, and then call Thea to arrange to meet her at the school, where Lizzie would explain everything.

Plan made, she prepared for the most vital explanation of her life.

Thea came powering towards Lizzie through the gates of the island's school. Throwing herself into her mother's arms, she exclaimed, 'You're wearing the *blue* dress today!' Thea's smile was sunny, but her sharp gaze missed nothing. 'You never wear dresses unless it's for a special occasion.'

Lizzie cheeks burned red with guilt beneath Thea's

scrutiny. 'I put the dress on for *you*. I went back to the restaurant specially—'

'You went *back*? From where?' Thea queried, fully in sleuth mode now. 'Where were you *before* the restaurant?'

'None of your business.'

Lizzie laughed. In spite of her tension, Thea's suspicious expression could always crack her up.

Thea narrowed her eyes. 'You were with *him*, weren't you?'

If only life was as simple as making a choice between a blue dress and a yellow dress, Lizzie thought, feeling a flutter of nerves now the moment had come to tell Thea the truth about her father.

'I love both dresses equally. You've got excellent taste.'

'That's not the question I asked you. What I want to know is, how did you get on with Damon?'

'Thea!' Lizzie tried and failed to be stern. 'As far as I can tell, he's a very nice man.'

'A *"very nice man"*?' Thea pulled a face.

'He's a good man,' Lizzie conceded carefully. She had to begin somewhere, but she could hardly pretend that she and Damon were bosom buddies right now.

'And…?' Thea pressed. 'Will you see him again soon?'

'I think it will be hard to avoid him on the island,' Lizzie said, speaking her thoughts out loud. 'But we should see him together next time—'

'No!' Thea cut in with disapproval. 'How is your

romance going to flourish with *me* there? You have to see him on your own.'

'I thought you liked him?'

'I do—but only if he makes you happy.'

'He enjoyed hearing you play,' Lizzie said, to break the sudden tension.

'He can come to a concert and hear the entire orchestra play,' Thea dismissed, clearly eager to move on the subject at the top of her agenda. 'It's *you* I'm worried about, not him.'

Lizzie's sinking feeling increased. 'We really need to talk about this.'

'Why?' Thea demanded.

'Because—'

Lizzie could see that Thea wasn't interested. Thea might be a musical prodigy, but she could be as difficult as any other ten-year-old child, and right now Thea's ears were closed to reason.

Lizzie still had to try. 'Because there's something I should have told you a long time ago. Why don't we sit in the shade and chat as we wait for the bus?'

Thea shrugged, but she plopped down on the bench next to Lizzie.

'So…you like Damon?' Lizzie began cautiously.

'A lot,' Thea said with a frown. 'We hit it off right away. But you already know that, so what's this about?'

Would Thea hate her when she told her? Would the reasons for her not telling her sooner about Damon matter, or would Thea believe that Lizzie had kept Damon away from her on purpose?

This wasn't about *her*, Lizzie concluded, or how *she* felt about the situation. This was about Thea and Damon, and Thea deserved to hear the truth.

'I'm glad you like Damon, because there's something I need to tell you about him—'

'He's asked you to marry him?' Thea exclaimed, leaping up from the bench.

'Not exactly,' Lizzie confessed. 'What I've got to tell you goes a lot further back than this trip to Greece.'

'Is he my father?'

Lizzie was stunned speechless. *'What?'* She felt as if she'd been punched.

'Well? Is he?' Thea demanded. 'Is Damon Gavros my father? Yes or no?'

'I wanted to break it to you gently—'

'There's only one way you can break news like this,' Thea insisted, 'and that's with a brass band. *Yes!*' she exulted, punching the air. 'I *knew* it!'

Lizzie put a steadying hand on Thea's arm, and for once wished someone would do the same for her. 'We're still all right, aren't we? I mean, you and me... the two of us?'

'Of course we are,' Thea confirmed impatiently. 'We'll carry on exactly as before. Won't we...?'

Lizzie would have walked over hot coals to take the look of uncertainty from Thea's face. 'Of course we will,' she said fiercely. 'No one's going to interfere in our lives.'

'Good,' Thea said. Her slender shoulders lifted in a shrug. 'He's never been around before, so why would he want to interfere now?'

'He *will* want to have some part in your life, Thea. He's your father, and you can't blame him for not being around when he's only just found out about you.'

'That doesn't give him any *rights* over me,' Thea said stubbornly. 'Believe me,' she said with agonising certainty, 'I'm quite an expert on this. Most of the kids at school have parents who are divorced, or about to be divorced—I listen to everything they say about it.'

'But I'm not married to Damon.'

'What difference does that make?' Thea demanded.

'I wanted to tell him as soon as I knew that I was pregnant with you, but I couldn't—'

'I don't care,' Thea declared, hugging Lizzie fiercely. 'I only care about *you*. I don't need anyone else,' she blurted on the brink of tears, instantly on her mother's side. 'We've done all right together, haven't we?'

'Of course we have.' Thea needed reassurance far more than she did, Lizzie thought as she dropped kisses on the top of Thea's head. 'And we'll continue to do all right, you and me.'

'Well, then…' Thea said, pulling back and looking up. '*Why* does he have to be part of my life?'

Holding Thea so she could look into her daughter's eyes, Lizzie said quietly, 'You've got nothing to worry about—*nothing*—do you hear me?'

'I hear you,' Thea said with absolute confidence.

This was not at all the way Lizzie had imagined things would turn out. Knowing Thea liked Damon, she had imagined Thea would be thrilled to learn Damon was her father. She had seemed thrilled, to begin with, but now Thea appeared to be more threatened than pleased by the news.

The important thing was that Thea understood that nothing would change between Thea and Lizzie because of these new circumstances.

'Why don't we meet him?' Lizzie suggested. 'You don't have to worry because I'll be there. You can get to know him slowly—in your own time. We both can, and then we'll take it from there. The one thing I promise is that you will *never* have to do anything you don't want to do.'

'Does that mean I can stay with you?' Thea blurted, her cheeks red and shiny with bottled-up emotion.

'Of *course* you can!' Lizzie drew Thea close.

'Because some of the girls at school never get to see their other parent, and I don't want that. I don't want to be away from you. I *love* you!' she exclaimed.

When Thea threw her arms around Lizzie, to give her the tightest hug ever, the dam finally broke and Lizzie cried.

He was waiting for Lizzie's call. *Take as much time as you need,* he'd told her. He'd step in when Thea was ready to meet him, and then Lizzie and he would have a discussion as to how to proceed from there.

He was confident all the problems could be ironed out. All that mattered to him, and to Lizzie too, was

Thea's happiness. He *did* have one irritation to handle, and that was the media who were sniffing around. His people had contacted him to warn him.

Rumours always followed him. He was one of the richest unmarried men in the world, so he supposed media interest was inevitable. He'd told his team to downplay it.

'If you do, they will,' he'd said.

'I doubt it, when Ms Montgomery has a dark-haired child who happens to be the spitting image of you *and* happens to be the child prodigy playing at your father's birthday party,' the head of his legal department had informed him.

'What if she *does* look like me?'

He mapped Thea's face in his mind. He couldn't believe he hadn't spotted the similarities between them before. He and Thea were obviously related, and that was a fact the press could hardly be expected to miss.

'There's bound to be speculation,' his lawyer advised. 'You'd do well to put the rumours to bed before they get out of control.'

'It's no one else's business,' Damon said coldly. 'I'm entitled to a private life and I intend to keep it that way: *private.*'

'You can't allow emotion to blind you to what might be going on here, Damon.'

'What are you suggesting?'

'Just that there are gold-diggers everywhere,' his lawyer continued doggedly.

'Are you referring to Ms Montgomery?'

'She *is* her father's daughter,' his lawyer said smoothly.

Damon bunched his fists. He knew the lawyer was only doing his job, and Damon had never wanted yes-men around him to boost his ego. The lawyer couldn't be faulted for braving his displeasure by giving him the plain truth.

'I'll give your advice some thought,' he conceded. 'In the meantime I expect you to keep the press off both Ms Montgomery's and her daughter's backs.'

'And yours,' his lawyer said.

'And mine,' Damon agreed wearily. If he didn't give the man one concession, who knew where the lawyer's enthusiasm for his job might lead?

CHAPTER TWELVE

SHE MUSTN'T HOPE for too much, Lizzie thought. This was just the first meeting between the three of them since Damon and Thea had learned the truth. Touch wood, it all seemed to be going well. Damon had invited them to his beach house, and Thea's eyes had rounded like golf balls as she'd stared around, but...

Why did there always have to be a but?

Because maybe she hadn't gone about this the right way. Perhaps she should have given Damon and Thea a chance to get to know each other before telling them that they were father and daughter.

Was there a right way to do this?

And then there were the practical points that they hadn't ironed out yet, Lizzie thought as Damon showed them around his glorious mansion. There were priceless rugs underfoot and striking works of art on the walls. The furniture was sleek and modern, and the house was kitted out with every luxury item imaginable—including an elegant grand piano in the hall beneath the sweeping marble staircase.

And still it echoed.

This was luxury on an unprecedented scale, but it told Lizzie nothing about Damon. There were no personal items, no photographs, no trophies, no memorabilia at all. And every footfall and whispered word between them travelled aimlessly around the vaulted space. It made Lizzie nostalgic for her cosy bedsit, where she had cuddled up on many a night with Thea.

This mansion was a sumptuous new build, waiting to have a family's personality imprinted upon it. And, even supposing things could be ironed out between Lizzie and Damon, how were they going to manage this? From being two separate units, could they become one?

What would be lost along the way? Lizzie thought as they walked from a cinema room to an indoor gym and a swimming pool complex, and on again to a full-scale library. Her independence? Lizzie wondered with a frisson of alarm. Or Thea's carefree take on life? Either way, she couldn't relax into the tour of this fabulous house and pretend she belonged there.

Thea had to be worried about the future too. She wasn't easily impressed—except maybe by a thrift shop find, or some priceless violin she'd seen in an auction house catalogue—and she had never lusted after riches. She had everything she needed, she would often tell Lizzie, but now Lizzie was beginning to wonder if Thea said it just to reassure her.

She would soon find out.

Lizzie's trust fund was heavily depleted, she accepted. Her father and stepmother had seen to that. The only time Lizzie felt secure was when *she* was in control. She might not have much, but what she had she'd earned, and she was confident she could make a safe and loving home for Thea.

Watching Thea and Damon together, the two of them so seemingly relaxed, made Lizzie edgy. She knew Thea well enough to know when Thea was being polite, rather than genuinely enthusiastic, and she suspected that was the case now, but she couldn't be sure until Thea expressed an opinion.

All she wanted was for Thea to be happy, but was this the way? Lizzie wondered as Thea reached out a hand, as if needing her mother's support. She crossed the room quickly to take hold of Thea's hand, sensing a need for reassurance beneath Thea's outwardly happy front.

Thea wasn't satisfied with holding hands, and threw herself into a hug, as if she needed to feel the security of her mother wrapped around her. 'Stay with me,' she insisted in a fierce whisper. 'You're part of this too.'

Was she? Lizzie wondered. Or was three a crowd?

He saw the concern on Lizzie's face and knew she was holding her feelings in, not wanting to influence Thea. They were both keen to keep this first meeting between the three of them as relaxed as possible.

How was it going so far?

Not so well, judging by Thea's white face.

'I'll leave you both to take a look around the house on your own,' he said. 'Take your time.'

'You're leaving us?' Thea said suspiciously.

There was an undercurrent behind those words that told him in no uncertain terms that it would take a lot more than one day to make up for eleven missing years.

'I'll take you back to the school when you're ready,' he reassured her. 'You two need some time alone to get used to the idea of having me in your life.'

'Do we *have* to?' he heard Thea ask Lizzie as he walked away.

Well, *that* was an unrivalled success, Lizzie thought cynically as Damon drove them back. If anything, things were tenser now than they had been before.

'Don't forget the party tomorrow,' Thea reminded Lizzie as Damon pulled up outside Thea's school.

'Party?' Lizzie exclaimed, and then she remembered. There was so much going on she could barely keep up.

'Tomorrow afternoon at the old gentleman's house.' Thea glanced at Damon. 'My…grandfather?' Thea frowned as she tested a word that could mean very little to her yet.

'That's right,' Damon confirmed. 'And my father can't wait to meet you.'

Things were moving fast, Lizzie reflected. Too fast, maybe, and none of it was easy for Thea.

'I'll be there,' she promised Thea.

She'd have to juggle her work schedule, as in spite of Iannis insisting she must take a holiday Lizzie had said that she'd help out with some of the last-minute preparations for the party.

Seeing Lizzie's concern, Damon stepped in. 'I spoke to Iannis on your behalf, so you can leave the restaurant early. I hope you don't mind?'

Before she could answer Thea piped up tensely, 'Are you going to organise *everything* in my mother's life now?'

'Thea!' Lizzie exclaimed, though she had to concede that Thea had a point.

'Thea's right,' Damon admitted, saving himself at the eleventh hour. 'I should have consulted you first, and I apologise. It's just that music is my father's joy, and he's very excited about tomorrow and the chance to meet you both.'

Thea wasn't taking things nearly as well as Lizzie had hoped. She would need a lot of reassurance going forward. And time. They both needed more time to get their heads around this new order.

'You don't have to work while you're here,' Damon told Lizzie, meaning to be helpful, no doubt, but only succeeding in garnering more black looks from Thea.

Thea wasn't shy in expressing her feelings on the subject. 'My mother *likes* to work. She tells me so all the time.'

Lizzie didn't comment on that, but she did voice her concerns. 'If I don't work, how can I support us both?'

Damon's expression was his answer. *He* would provide for them. But that didn't suit Lizzie.

Meanwhile Thea's head was snapping from side to side, like a spectator at a tennis match, with an expression on her face that clearly said, *See? I told you what parents were like*—which was the last thing Lizzie had wanted.

When Thea had climbed out of the SUV outside the school, Lizzie took off her seat belt. 'I'll get out here too,' she told Damon. 'Thanks for the lift. I'll catch the bus back to the restaurant.'

It would be a relief to leave the tension in the enclosed cabin of the SUV behind, but that was only a minor reason for her taking this decision. She wanted to reassure Thea, and that was more important than anything. She also wanted to tell Damon that this wouldn't work if he insisted on acting without listening.

But her priority was Thea, whose sigh of relief when Damon drove away was almost as deep as Lizzie's.

The party at the grand old mansion was in full swing by the time Lizzie and Thea arrived. Lizzie had managed to reassure Thea a little by this point, and they both found it impossible not to smile when they were welcomed to the Gavros family home with the warmest of greetings by the man they now knew was Thea's grandfather.

The man her father had defrauded, Lizzie remembered, incredulous that *anyone* could have a heart big enough to put the past in the past and give them such a warm welcome.

The large, impressive house was not what Lizzie had expected either. Far from being a stuffy museum, it was a cluttered home, slightly shabby, with dogs running around and cats commanding all the best chairs.

'Thea!' Thea's grandfather grasped her hands. 'I've heard so much about you. Welcome to our home,' he said, shaking Thea's hand formally—to give him chance to study Thea's face without being too obvious about it, Lizzie thought. '*Your* home too now,' he advised Thea gently.

As Lizzie watched on she felt a pang as Damon's father continued to look at Thea as if he were drinking in every last detail, thirsty for knowledge of his granddaughter. Lizzie's fears that Thea would remain tense, maybe even a little surly, quickly disappeared. They had both been reassured by the old gentleman's warmth and his genuine manner. Thea had completely relaxed, and was returning his smile.

'I'm very pleased to be here,' Thea said politely, studying her grandfather with matching interest.

'Welcome home,' he declared, turning to Lizzie.

'Thank you.'

Lizzie was floored by the welcome. Damon's father had so many reasons to hate everything about her family, and yet he was greeting them with such warmth. Her emotions surged, regret and wistfulness competing as she thought back to another time, when her mother had been alive and they had lived in a loving and slightly chaotic home just like this.

'I hardly dare to shake your hand, young lady,' Thea's grandfather was confiding in Thea. 'In case I damage it!' he explained, which made them both laugh.

Infected by their *joie de vivre*, Lizzie relaxed enough to laugh too, while Thea insisted, 'My hand's made of tougher stuff than that.'

'And is your mother made of the same *tough stuff*?' Thea's grandfather asked, turning his wise gaze on Lizzie.

'My mother's the best mother in the world—*and* the most beautiful!'

'Thea—' Lizzie protested. Her cheeks fired red. 'We mustn't hog all of Kirio Gavros's time. He does have other guests.'

'But none as important as you,' Damon's father assured Lizzie. 'Your daughter speaks with passion. You're a very lucky woman. Please,' he added, gesturing towards an open door through which they could see the garden, 'enjoy the sunshine and the music. There's an ice cream cart, Thea—and it looks as if your friends are here to escort you,' he exclaimed as a group from the youth orchestra crowded round.

'You're very generous. Thank you,' Lizzie said warmly, turning to go.

'No. *You* are generous,' Thea's grandfather argued softly. 'You didn't need to come here. You didn't need to allow Thea to come here. So I thank you from the bottom of my heart.'

Hearing the break in his voice, Lizzie turned. 'Thank you for inviting us.' It still didn't seem enough after what her father had put him through, and impulsively she went back to kiss Damon's father on both cheeks.

'Don't be a stranger, Lizzie,' he whispered. 'The

past is the past. Remember that always, and never let the past hold you back.'

When she finally broke away she had tears in her eyes. 'Thea—what do you say?' she called out, needing a few moments to rein in her emotions.

'Thank you!' Thea called back to her grandfather with a happy wave, before her friends dragged her away.

'Go and enjoy yourself,' Damon's father insisted, chivvying Lizzie across the hall with great warmth.

She had a lot to think about by the time she left the cool of the hall for the heat of the blazing sun.

'Over here, Mama—here, beneath the trees.'

Shading her eyes, Lizzie saw that with unerring good sense Thea and her friends had set up camp beneath the generous canopy of a jacaranda tree.

An elderly lady was introducing herself to the children as Lizzie approached. Was this humorous, twinkly sparrow of a woman Damon's mother? Lizzie wondered. Somehow she'd expected to find a tall, elegant, possibly fearsome lady, rather than this instantly likeable person.

She missed her own mother so badly for a moment she had to pause to let her emotions subside before she could walk up and introduce herself.

Damon's mother took her hand in both of hers. 'Welcome, Lizzie,' she said, smiling. She scanned Lizzie's face and her smile widened. 'We're so very pleased to have you here.'

This was said with such warmth that Lizzie's eyes brimmed a second time.

'Anything the two of you want,' Damon's mother added, glancing at Thea, 'please know that you only have to ask.'

'Thank you.'

This was so much more than Lizzie had hoped for. And the sincerity of Damon's parents said a lot about Damon. No wonder he'd worked so hard to put things right for them, to ensure that their retirement was worry-free. They all had a lot of lost time to make up for, but for the first time Lizzie wanted to believe that it might be possible.

'I'm glad you came.'

Damon's voice was deep and husky, and Lizzie tingled all over to hear him so close behind her. His mother had moved closer to the children to talk to them, leaving the two of them alone.

'Shall we?' he asked, leading Lizzie away from the happy tableau of Thea and her grandmother and Thea's friends.

Her body heated beneath his dark gaze. His sensuality was overpowering. She was spellbound by his sexual charisma, Lizzie concluded, and she badly needed not to be if she was to think clearly.

Damon halted at the side of a swimming pool, beneath the shade of an awning, where they could talk discreetly.

'Your parents couldn't have been more welcoming. You're a very lucky man.'

'They worked hard to make me what I am,' he countered dryly. 'And I didn't make it easy for them.'

She was sure he had not.

'This is a wonderful occasion…'

Lizzie's mouth dried as she gazed around. She felt threatened by this very different, very privileged lifestyle. Even her father, at the height of his showing off, had never lived in a property remotely comparable to this majestic home.

Bunting fluttered from the huge white marquee set in the centre of a flawless emerald-green lawn, while the surrounding garden was like a park full of colour, with ponds and streams and majestic fountains flowing. Behind this the grand old house watched over the proceedings with the elegance of centuries emblazoned on its grey stone. Lizzie wouldn't blame Thea if she was tempted to throw aside their bedsit for the chance to live somewhere like this.

'Everything needs careful handling,' Damon said, as if reading her mind.

She turned to look at him. 'Of course it does.' She followed his gaze to where Thea was chatting happily with his parents, both of whom had now joined the group of children.

'Shall we?' Damon suggested again, angling his chin towards the house.

She almost didn't want to leave. It was as if she feared losing her place in Thea's affections, was worried that she might be pushed out to make room for a new family and a new life.

'Now?' he prompted.

Why could neither of them be honest about their feelings? Lizzie wondered. The sexual tension between her and Damon was as fierce as ever, and they never seemed to have any problem expressing that, but where emotions were concerned they were both equally skilled at hiding them.

It was a lot to take in, Lizzie reasoned, but decided to break the ice first.

'I wish your parents hadn't been left out of the loop for so long,' she admitted as Damon held open the door into the main house for her.

'They do too,' he said frankly. 'But what can't be changed must be accepted and dealt with. The main thing is that they're both overjoyed to discover they have a granddaughter at this stage of their lives. Thea's happiness is all they care about. They have no resentment. In fact, far from it. They're grateful to you. They can't thank you enough. They know you've had a difficult life, and they also know I didn't make it any easier for you. They certainly don't pity you,' he added, anticipating her possible reaction. 'If anything, they admire you more than they can say. Come in,' he added, beckoning her into the house when she hesitated on the threshold.

She looked around with interest as Damon led the way through a hallway packed with a selection of boots and gardening tools to open the door on to a comfortably ramshackle sitting room. Everything she looked at wore the patina of age with grace. There were chunks out of chair legs where dogs had chewed, and threaded curtains where cats had climbed, and in spite of everything going on in their lives Lizzie felt wistful, knowing Damon had grown up in a *real* family home—which was exactly what she'd always dreamed of for Thea.

'You've never been frightened of change before, Lizzie.'

'Is that how it looks to you?' She laughed softly. 'I *am* afraid of change,' she admitted. 'I just hide it well.'

'And now I'm in your life you know there's more change coming?'

She shivered involuntarily. That sounded like a threat. 'There's change, and then there's your billionaire lifestyle,' she admitted. 'It might take Thea and me a long time to get used to that.'

'I think you'd both adapt pretty quickly.'

'We might not *want* to,' Lizzie pointed out. 'Thea still has to get used to the idea of having a father in her life and I'll resent losing my independence. I know you have a lot,' she said, with magnificent understatement, 'but you can't *buy* Thea or me. Nor can you direct a child to love or even accept you. That will take time, and even then there are no guarantees. I'm sorry.' She really was. 'You'll just have to wait and see.'

'That's not my way,' Damon assured her.

'Then you might want to rethink *your way*,' Lizzie countered, as mildly as she could. 'Thea is a young person with an independent mind—as I think you've seen for yourself.'

'And what about you, Lizzie?'

'The same goes for me—though my primary concern is Thea, and any decision I make will be based on that.'

'It's not my intention to steal Thea from you,' Damon was quick to add.

Then why even mention it? Lizzie thought.

CHAPTER THIRTEEN

THEY MADE ARRANGEMENTS for more meetings between the three of them, and then Lizzie left Damon so she could go and find Thea. The rest of the afternoon passed happily, if a little tensely, at least for Lizzie, but without incident. She stayed for the first part of the concert in the evening, but as Thea wasn't playing in the second half Lizzie returned to the restaurant and took the opportunity, while it was closed, to perform a stock-take and do a deep clean.

It was a relief to work with her hands and take her mind off everything else. Even with the wonderful Gavros grandparents, the warmest of welcomes, and Damon's obvious intention to make things right for Thea, Lizzie couldn't shake a feeling of uneasiness.

Maybe it was his mention of not stealing Thea from her. Why had that thought even entered his mind? The future was so hard to visualise, and that was what worried her more than anything.

Work saved her. It always had. She could feel her pulse steadying even as she mopped the floor. Work was the rock she had always clung to. It was the re-

assurance she needed to know that she would always
be able to support Thea and herself.

'No wonder my cousin loves you,' Iannis commented when he returned from the party to find his
kitchen in tip-top condition and a list neatly drawn
up ready for his visit to the wholesalers the next day.
'*Everyone* loves you, Lizzie.'

'So long as *you* do,' she teased Iannis, and then
tensed at the sound of a powerful engine drawing
closer.

'Uh-oh,' Iannis murmured. 'I'd better make myself scarce.'

'Please don't—'

Too late. Iannis had already disappeared into the
pantry.

Lizzie glanced outside to confirm her suspicions.
Damon, driving a stylish black Aston Martin DB9,
had just opened the driver's door and climbed out.
How was she supposed to stop every atom in her
being yearning for him? Maybe she'd never get that
under control. It wasn't fair for anyone to look so quite
so stunning this late at night.

She smoothed her hair self-consciously, knowing
that she certainly didn't look her best, and that even
her best could never compete with Damon's darkly
glittering glamour. He looked incredible, wearing
nothing more than a pair of snug-fitting jeans and
a slate-blue linen shirt with the sleeves rolled back.

'Why are you here?' She lowered her arms, realising that she was hugging herself defensively as he
jogged up the steps. His arrival had charged the air

with electricity, changing the mood—her mood, specifically. Damon changed everything.

'Hello to you too,' he remarked dryly. 'Why am I here? To take you on a moonlit drive.'

Lizzie shook her head. 'I don't think so. It's far too late.'

'I don't know what kind of carriages you're used to, Cinderella, but I can assure you mine is in no danger of turning into a pumpkin at midnight.'

'Less of the Cinderella, please. I'm all out of glass slippers.' He was close enough for her to feel his heat warming her, and to smell the faint scent of his exclusive cologne.

'We need to talk,' Damon insisted.

'I agree,' she said. 'But why now?'

'Why not now?' Damon argued. 'We can't keep putting this off. Neither of us wants Thea to be confused, and she will be if we don't get things straightened out between us.'

Thea was the magic word. He must know it would work. She could see the change in his eyes when she made her decision. 'I'd need to go and get changed first.'

'Okay.' Damon shrugged. 'You do that and I'll wait.'

'I'll be as quick as I can.'

And only because it involved Thea, Lizzie thought as she raced upstairs to change out of her work clothes, with her heart hammering off the scale.

He drew the car to a halt on top of the cliff overlooking the bay, where there was no sound other than the cicadas chittering and the ocean breathing rhythmically below. Lizzie was freshly showered. He could still smell the shower gel she'd used. She'd changed into casual jeans and a top, but she was still strung out.

'You need to relax,' he told her.

'How can I, when everything I care about is under threat?'

'Not from me.'

She didn't say anything, but her silence was a response in itself.

'So, what do you want to discuss?' she said at last. 'Because I think I need to see a lawyer before we decide to do anything.'

'Does it have to be so formal between us?'

She turned to stare at him steadily. 'Yes. I think it does.'

'Would it upset you to know that my asking you out tonight isn't *all* about custody and visitation rights?'

She stared at him blankly. 'I don't understand.'

'I needed to see you,' Damon said bluntly, 'and not to talk—not tonight.'

'You've got me here on false pretences,' Lizzie protested, clearly not impressed. 'We can talk, or you can take me back. Please,' she added as a tense afterthought.

'You have to have a life too.'

'You're my counsellor now?' She didn't wait for him to answer. 'For your information, I already have a life.'

'*Do* you? Do you allow yourself to?'

She laughed that off. 'I have the life I want.'

He let that pass, and reassured her by explaining that he wanted to get to know Thea slowly, and always with Lizzie around to help break any possible tension between them.

'I know this is going to take time. And I know you think I'm impatient, which I am, but this is something different. I do understand that.'

'For which I'm very grateful,' she said.

He smiled at her spikiness. It reminded him of the old Lizzie, full of fire and defiance. He knew that Lizzie was still in there somewhere. It was just that this Lizzie had devoted her life to Thea at the expense of her own.

'I want the two of you to come back to Greece and spend more time here. So you can both get used to the idea of having more options,' he explained.

That was as far as he thought it wise to take it while Lizzie was so tense and insistent upon seeing everything as a threat.

'Yes,' she agreed, and this time she didn't look away, but held his gaze steadily.

A different type of tension had been building between them while they'd been talking. Being enclosed in the confines of the car had something to do with it, and that tension would need an outlet soon.

'What?' he prompted, sensing that something else was troubling Lizzie.

'Your life will remain largely unchanged,' she pointed out, 'while ours will be massively changed.'

'You don't think my life will change? Of *course*

my life will change. How could it ever be the same again? And your life will be better—and easier,' he insisted.

'I won't take your money!' she exclaimed. 'You seem to think that money is the answer to everything, but it can't even come close.'

'I have a daughter to think about now,' he argued firmly. 'Where are you going?' he asked as Lizzie fumbled with the door handle.

'Don't!' she warned when he leaned across to stop her. 'I need to get out and have some space to think.'

'On a cliff-edge?' he cautioned.

She had to get out of the car—she couldn't think straight with Damon so close and her whole being yearning for him. It could only lead to disaster if she stayed. How *could* she trust Damon? How could she trust *anyone*?

Part of her wanted to go back to the enclosed world she'd built with Thea, while the other part of her knew that that wouldn't be fair to Thea, or even healthy for Lizzie. First and foremost she had to calm down. She'd never been a coward. She'd always faced things head-on.

She turned to face Damon. They were still touching. His hand was resting on hers as he tried to stop her getting out of the car, and his body was pressed tightly against her. Fighting him was never going to be a good idea. They didn't have to do much to light the fuse between them, and there was far too much at stake now. Combine that with the passion Lizzie had been bottling up inside for eleven years, and this was a recipe for disaster.

'Have you ever made out in a car?' Damon asked, smiling faintly at her.

'No. And I've no intention of ever doing so,' she assured him, pulling back.

'Really?' Damon murmured, sounding not in the least bit dismayed 'Sometimes I find a release of tension helps to clear the mind.'

'I bet you do,' she agreed dryly, straightening her clothes.

She'd barely done that when Damon adjusted her seat in a way that made it instantly flat, and she shrieked with surprise.

'Well, it's definitely possible,' he observed, frowning as if he didn't *know* that throwing that lever would result in landing Lizzie on her back.

'I'll just have to take your word for it,' she said tensely, starting to struggle up.

'You can do more than that…'

As she was about to discover.

'Brute,' she whispered shakily as Damon dropped kisses on her neck. 'This is so totally unfair.'

'I suppose it is,' he agreed, working magic with his hands.

When Damon's mouth closed on hers and his tongue plundered all the dark, hidden places, she felt the response spread throughout her body like wildfire. Moving into the footwell on his knees in front of her, he nudged her legs apart and continued with the teasing.

'I think you like this,' he observed as his hands worked lightly, skilfully and steadily.

'You on your knees in front of me? What's not to like?' she somehow managed to gasp out.

He laughed, and she closed her eyes so she could only feel and listen to the sounds of pleasure.

He swiftly disposed of her jeans and underwear and, lifting her legs, rested them on the wide spread of his shoulders, giving her just enough time to grab hanks of his hair before plunging deep.

The sensation was incredible. There might be very little room for manoeuvre, with Damon's powerful frame taking up all the space, but he didn't need it to prove how proficient he could be even in the confines of the car.

'*Theos!* I've missed you,' he growled.

'It hasn't been that long—'

'Too long,' he argued fiercely.

She wasn't going to argue as he continued to move in the way she loved. Damon was a master of pleasure, and he knew her body far too well. He brought her to the edge in moments, and he kept her hovering until he commanded, 'Don't hold on.'

She needed no encouragement, and fell instantly, noisily and gratefully. Each pleasure wave stunned her, and she gorged herself on that pleasure. It was only when they both surfaced, with the moon acting as a spotlight, that they could see how far the car had moved forward.

'I'm really glad you didn't park on the edge,' Lizzie commented with relief.

Damon laughed, and then they were both laughing, still entwined in each other's arms.

If only life could be this simple and go on like this for ever, Lizzie thought.

'Could it be that you're starting to trust me?' Damon asked, and she levelled a long, considering look on his face.

Trust was such a big issue for Lizzie, and she didn't answer right away. Then, 'Yes, I am,' she said at last.

Drawing her into his arms, Damon held her and kissed her. 'Don't ever lose the faith again.'

'I won't,' she promised, snuggling close.

She only wished the little niggle of doubt inside her would go away.

'I *know* we'll move forward from here,' Damon said confidently.

'Not over the edge of the cliff, I hope?'

He pulled back to smile down at her and she smiled contentedly.

'I'm being serious,' Damon insisted. 'I hope you're not suggesting that I don't play fair?'

'Well, *do* you?' It was Lizzie's turn to lift her head and stare at Damon.

'I play to win,' he said.

CHAPTER FOURTEEN

NOTHING WAS EVER completely straightforward, Lizzie thought as she climbed into Damon's SUV outside the restaurant the next morning. Still intensely aware of him, thanks to a night that had left her wanting more, they were now on their way to the school to pick up Thea—just as regular parents picked up their children.

They had planned a return to the beach house to try and make a better go of things than they had last time. Thea would have a home in Greece as well as in England, Damon had told Lizzie before he'd dropped her off last night at the restaurant, and a music studio all her own. That had really chimed with Lizzie. Yes, she might have everything to lose—including her heart, to Damon—but she couldn't keep an opportunity like that out of Thea's reach.

'Good night's sleep?' he asked dryly as they turned onto the main road.

'Yes. You?' she asked in an innocent tone, knowing she hadn't slept a wink.

She'd told Damon to drop her off at the restaurant the previous night, but he'd wanted to take her back to the beach house, where they would be able to make love in comfort. She had shied away from that level of involvement. To wake up beside Damon and find herself wanting things she couldn't have wouldn't help anyone, and she needed to keep a clear head if she was to try and work out how to keep things running smoothly for Thea in their utterly changed lives.

Thea was waiting for them outside the school, and everything seemed to be going well to begin with. Thea was excited at the thought of going to the beach, and Damon was buzzing too.

'I've got a gift for you,' he told Thea, the moment they walked through the door of his beachside mansion.

'For *me*?' Thea said excitedly as Damon led the way into the house.

She was still a child, Lizzie thought, feeling more than ever protective. Thea loved presents, and Lizzie couldn't afford nearly enough of them.

Damon took them into the room that Lizzie had already planned in her fantasy world would be Thea's music studio. There was the grand piano, in one corner, and a new addition...a violin case...was resting on the piano stool.

'It's for you,' Damon explained when Thea remained hovering uncertainly by the door. 'The violin's for *you*, Thea. Call it an early Christmas present.'

'It's only June,' Thea said in a small voice.

That short comment was the only warning Lizzie

needed that things weren't all right with Thea. She knew her daughter's moods.

Thea proved her right by being uncharacteristically subdued as she walked across the room. Reaching out one small hand, she tentatively trailed her fingertips across the violin case.

'Well? Aren't you going to open it?' Lizzie asked, glancing anxiously at Damon, who had also tensed, she noticed.

Thea didn't say anything. She snapped the catches, lifted the lid—and stood back.

'Is something wrong?' Damon asked.

Thea was pale when she turned around, and instead of saying any of the things they might have expected, asked simply, 'Is everything going to change now?'

'No, of course not!' Rushing to Thea's side, Lizzie gave her a hug.

'What do you mean, Thea?' Damon asked quietly.

They looked at each other over Thea's head.

Breaking free of Lizzie, Thea explained, 'I know this is a very valuable instrument, and I know I should be grateful. It's a very thoughtful gift…and I thank you,' she added in a small voice. 'But it's far too good for me—especially when I don't even know if I'll still be playing the violin when I grow up.'

This hammer-blow struck at Lizzie's heart. It took all she'd got not to show how shocked she was by Thea's remark. She couldn't believe she'd never sensed this doubt in Thea before, and felt immediately guilty. Had she urged Thea down the wrong path? She couldn't put her hand on her heart and be sure of anything.

Even Damon seemed lost for words for once, and Thea hadn't finished yet.

'My mother worked very hard to buy me my first full-sized violin,' she explained patiently to Damon, with all the seriousness a ten-year-old could muster. 'She worked long hours and put small payments down until she'd paid enough for me to take the violin home. We'd seen the violin I wanted in a pawnshop window, and my mother begged the owner of the shop not to sell it to anyone else,' she explained. 'And there's something else… Can I tell him?'

'No,' Lizzie said, flashing a warning glance at Thea.

'Tell me what?' Damon prompted.

'Nothing,' Lizzie said quickly.

'You speak for your daughter now?'

For an instant Thea looked as if she'd like to kill Damon and, pleased as she was at the way her daughter had leapt to her defence, Lizzie knew this was hardly helpful when it came to bringing the three of them closer.

'Thea, please…' she cautioned gently, but Thea refused to be stopped.

'My mother had to sell things at the pawnshop,' Thea said bluntly, with an angry frown on her face as she remembered. 'Special things she really cared about. She did that so she could buy me all the extras I needed at school and pay for my violin. Why would I want another instrument when mine was bought with so much love?'

A long silence followed.

'Maybe when you're older?' Lizzie suggested in the awkward break.

'No,' Thea argued. 'If I play the violin at all, no other violin could ever mean as much to me. The only reason I play so well is because *you* bought my instrument for me. I might not even *want* to be a professional musician when I'm older. I might want to be an airline pilot, or an engineer—or maybe a comedian?' Thea raised her chin as she considered this last option.

'You can be anything you want to be,' Lizzie agreed.

Damon's face remained expressionless throughout, and Lizzie almost felt sorry for him. Once again it came down to the fact that not everything could be bought with money and a gap of eleven years could not be easily filled. That was something they both had to come to terms with.

'You're right, Thea,' Damon conceded. 'I should have asked what you wanted before I bought the violin.'

'No—it's good. It's lovely,' Thea said quickly, obviously eager to make amends.

She wasn't a cruel child. Thea was sensitive, which showed in her music, and she knew when someone was hurt. Lizzie had never been prouder of Thea than she was right now.

'Can you return it to the shop and get your money back?' Thea suggested with concern.

'I'm sure I can,' Damon said confidently.

They were all on a steep learning curve, and no

doubt they'd all make more mistakes, Lizzie thought as Thea turned to her. 'You're not upset that I might not want to be a professional violinist, are you?' she asked, staring into Lizzie's eyes with concern.

'It's your life,' Lizzie said gently. 'You have to follow your star.'

'I knew you'd understand!' Thea exclaimed, relaxing into a happy smile at once. 'And you *will* get your mother's wedding ring back one day, I promise. *I'll* get it back for you— Oops.' She glanced at Damon, and then at Lizzie. 'I shouldn't have said that, should I?'

Lizzie reassured Thea with a smile. This was exactly what she'd dreaded—that Thea would end up like Lizzie, feeling guilty all the time. So what if her secret was out? Thea hadn't meant any harm by it. And it was the truth. There had never been enough money for Lizzie to buy back her mother's ring.

She wanted Damon to know that she appreciated his gesture—that she understood that he was trying to make up for all the lost years by wrapping every birthday and Christmas present he'd missed into one fabulous gift. He'd done a really great thing, and for all the right reasons, but because he didn't know Thea his gesture had fallen flat.

A week later Damon watched Lizzie and Thea's plane take off into the mid-afternoon sky on its way to London. He'd worked hard in the intervening days to make up for his gaffe with the violin, and his reward had been seeing Thea gradually return to the ease they'd shared before they'd known they were father and daughter.

He understood Thea's stout defence of her mother, and could only admire her for it. As Lizzie had said, it would take time to reassure Thea that things would be better now, not worse. And he was prepared to wait for as long as it took. For the first time in his life he couldn't afford to be impatient. Thea was too important for him to get this wrong.

It was only when he turned to go to his car that he realised how alone he felt now they'd gone. Had he always felt this way? The answer was an unequivocal no. He'd never known what he was missing before today.

He stood by the car, gazing up at the sky until the jet carrying Lizzie and Thea away became a silver dot before disappearing. He and Lizzie had made certain decisions, which included taking things slowly, but those decisions, so carefully made, didn't feel right to him now.

Climbing into the car, he released the handbrake and pulled away from the kerb.

Would Lizzie ever return to Greece?

He was so busy scrutinising the sky in the direction Lizzie's jet had taken that he almost drove into a ditch. He adjusted his steering fast.

Maybe it was time to adjust his life and his thinking too.

Thea had buried herself in a book for the duration of the flight home, giving Lizzie plenty of time to think. Everything had been almost perfect during their last few days on the island, she mused. If there *was* a problem it was Lizzie, with her courage for others and caution for herself. She had never used to be like that, but she had to keep everything safe and steady for Thea.

Was Damon right in saying she should have a life too? Did Thea deserve a mother who could never pull back and see what was under her nose? *Was* she smothering Thea? Was that why Thea had said what she'd said about not necessarily following a career as a musician when she was older?

On the other hand Damon had got things right these past few days. His family had been more involved with Thea, and the more Lizzie had got to know them, the more she'd come to believe that having them in their lives could only be a good thing for Thea.

Now there was just the problem of Lizzie and Damon, and where *they* went from here…if they went anywhere.

There were grey clouds over London as the plane came in to land. The aircraft hit turbulence and juddered suddenly and Lizzie gasped and gripped the armrest.

'What's wrong?' Thea asked.

'Nothing. Everything's perfect.'

So why did she have to try so hard to convince herself that this was true? Couldn't she do as Damon asked and trust him for once?

Lizzie couldn't even put a name to the doubt inside her, except to say that it refused to go away. It was a relief when the plane broke through the clouds and they landed safely.

Lizzie kissed Thea goodbye at the gates of the school boarding house where Thea stayed during term time. Thea was popular, which made parting easier, though it was never easy for Lizzie on the bus ride home. She always felt sad when she left Thea at school—and especially now, when she knew that Thea wasn't wholly committed to a future as a professional musician.

Some fairly big decisions would have to be made soon. If Thea *did* decide to become a day pupil Lizzie would be the happiest mother alive. The complications it would throw up would just have to be worked through, like everything else. Flexi-working, Lizzie thought as she put the key in the door. That was the answer.

She'd just have to hope she could earn enough money working part-time and still be available when Thea needed her. She'd always found a solution in the past, so there was no reason to suppose that she couldn't do so again.

The house that encompassed her bedsit was empty…echoing and empty. The owners were obviously away.

Shaking off the feeling of loneliness, Lizzie picked up her mail and wheeled her suitcase into her room. A coffee first, and then she'd look at the important things.

There was a lot of mail to throw away first—fly-

ers, menus from the local take-away restaurants—
and then one very official-looking envelope, with
the name of a legal firm that shot fear into her heart
stamped in confident black letters across the top.

Coffee would have to wait, she decided as she
turned the envelope over in her hands. The last time
she'd heard the name of this law firm had been eleven
years ago, in court.

Might as well get it over with…

She didn't even pause to shrug off her jacket. She
just ripped the thick velum envelope open and took
out the letter. She unfolded it and started to read.

For once she was glad of the small room and the
bed immediately behind her as she sank down, trembling.

Was this what Damon meant by trust? Trust was
as ephemeral as a puff of smoke. Trust was a state of
mind for fools and romantics. And she had proved to
be both, Lizzie concluded as she read the letter again.

Acting on behalf of Damon Gavros, the lawyer was
asking—no, *demanding*—that a DNA test to establish Thea's genetic link to Damon must be undertaken
at a clinic of his choice at the earliest opportunity.

> *You will appreciate that my client is an ex-*
> *tremely wealthy man who must take sensible*
> *precautions. A legal paternity test can settle*
> *matters such as child support, child custody,*
> *visitation dispute, and inheritance issues, and*
> *will satisfy immigration requirements.*
>
> *A strict chain of custody under the supervi-*

*sion of this firm will ensure that samples taken
remain in compliance with all legal require-
ments—*

There was a lot more legalese, but she'd read
enough. It wasn't so much the request made by Damon's legal representatives, but the fact that she'd
been with Damon only a few hours before the letter had arrived and he hadn't thought to mention it.

Holding the letter, she sat on the bed with her head
bowed, thinking. It had never once occurred to her
that Damon would doubt Thea's parentage. She'd been
a virgin when they'd met—which he knew—and she
hadn't slept with anyone else—which he also knew.
Thea was *Damon's* child. There wasn't the smallest
doubt about it. And yet he still wanted proof?

*Maybe he thought the apple hadn't fallen far from
the tree.*

Lizzie blazed inwardly as she thought about that.
She took after her mother—as Thea did—not her
weak and imprudent father.

The main thing now was to protect Thea at all
costs. She must remain calm. She wouldn't allow the
test to happen. She had that power at least.

Even as she thought about it Lizzie felt her spirits
reviving. Thea would *not* be made to think there was
something wrong with her. And as for this lawyer
suggesting that a man as rich as Croesus must take
sensible precautions—perhaps Damon should have
thought of that when they'd made love.

Yes, she'd been willing enough, and, yes, he'd used

protection. But there had been a lot of sex that night, and maybe Damon hadn't been as meticulous as he'd thought. She took responsibility too, and now it was up to her to protect Thea from every possible hurt.

But what angered Lizzie most was the way this had been done. What would have been so hard about Damon telling her to her face that he wanted a DNA test?

Her offer to give him time to integrate into Thea's life was a joke now. She'd had no idea that love came with a price tag attached. It seemed to her that Damon was only interested in protecting his precious bank balance. And how would Thea feel, having started to build a tentative relationship with her father only to be told that he needed proof that he was her father?

If new love was a tender green shoot, Damon had just trampled it. Thea would be heartbroken if she ever learned about this. Lizzie had never forgotten the feelings of abandonment she had suffered as a child, and was determined that Thea would *never* suffer anything similar.

It all boiled down to one simple question: was Damon Gavros fit to be Thea's father?

Going on this evidence? *No.* He was *not.* Either Damon wanted to build a relationship with Thea or he didn't, and no amount of test results could change that.

The twenty-four hours before he'd been able to file a flight plan to London had left him in a state of advanced impatience and frustration. He headed straight for the Greek restaurant when he arrived in the city, where he found Stavros in the kitchen. There was no sign of Lizzie, and his welcome from Stavros was unusually cool.

'She's at home,' Stavros told him, in what Damon could only describe as a hostile tone. 'Recovering,' Stavros added significantly.

'Is she ill?' Alarm iced him.

'Heartsick,' Stavros said, staring pointedly at the door.

He took the hint. 'Okay, I get it. I'm going. Her address…?'

'If Lizzie had wanted you to know where she lives she would have given you her address,' Stavros informed him with a cold stare.

'I need that address *now*,' he insisted. 'And her mobile number, in case she's not there.'

'Can't your *lawyer* supply those?'

'My lawyer?' Damon frowned. 'What's my lawyer got to do with this?'

The way Stavros shrugged sent an icy finger of suspicion tracking down Damon's spine. The head lawyer on his legal team had a notoriously itchy trigger finger, and remembering the warning he'd given Damon set alarm bells ringing.

'Lizzie's address and number *now*,' he urged, in a tone that even the loyal Stavros couldn't ignore. 'Please,' he added, consciously softening his tone as the restaurateur stared at him belligerently.

Finding Lizzie was too important to risk on a point of pride. He had only realised what he'd lost when she'd left the island. They'd started to build something that in these very early stages might all too easily be destroyed. He had to stop that happening *now*—not some time in the future. There had been too much delay on both parts.

'If you care anything at all for Lizzie and Thea, please help me,' he begged. When Stavros blinked with surprise at his obvious distress, he added, 'I *have* to see her now.'

Rather reluctantly Stavros jotted something down on a scrap of paper. When he handed it over Damon was reminded that he took too much for granted. He shouldn't have to ask for Lizzie's address. He should *know* her address. If he cared anything for Lizzie and Thea he should have every detail concerning them locked down.

He had lived a charmed life up to now, Damon concluded as he thanked Stavros and stowed the precious piece of paper in his pocket.

He left the restaurant at speed and leapt into his car. Tapping Lizzie's address into the sat nav, he sped away. The head of his legal team had always acted in Damon's best interests before—as seen through his legal eyes—and in fairness Damon expected him to take the initiative at his level, rather than always wait for instruction. But there were some things that should be out of his lawyer's control—and this was one of them. If he didn't make things right straight away Damon would be a man who had learned too late how much he had to lose.

He headed towards the suburbs at speed. An

adored only son, he had entered the world on a cloud of privilege, and that sense of entitlement had continued on into his adult life. He saw. He seized. He conquered and his empire grew.

He'd always been able to see the path ahead clearly—until Lizzie had come into his life and changed the rules. Lizzie had changed everything, and he couldn't even be sure if she would agree to see him now.

Only one thing was certain in his immediate future, and that was that it was going to be the fight of his life.

CHAPTER FIFTEEN

DAMON? HOW COULD *Damon* possibly be parked outside her door?

For a moment Lizzie couldn't catch her breath, she was so shocked. *Damon had followed her to London!* She hadn't even had a chance to collect her thoughts properly after receiving his lawyer's letter yesterday—other than to call a family solicitor and make an appointment.

She froze behind the shutters of her room as she checked out the sleek black car parked outside the front door. The windows were tinted, so she couldn't see the driver, but she knew who it was. There was only one man who changed his car as often as his shirt, and always for a newer, sleeker model.

Better to have this out with him now, she concluded as she glanced at the letter, still lying on the table by the phone where she'd left it. Stavros had given her some time off, allowing her the chance to think her way through this nightmare. He'd winkled the truth out of her when he'd heard the tension in her voice.

Stavros had been furious too. He couldn't believe it of Damon, he'd said, adding that any lawyer sent by Damon Gavros would have to come through *him* first.

From being a wily matchmaker, Stavros had turned on a sixpence into Lizzie's staunchest defender. He'd wanted to send his wife over right away, to comfort her, but Lizzie had said she could handle things on her own. And she *would*, Lizzie determined.

She drew a deep, steadying breath before opening the front door. This wasn't the first hurdle she'd faced by any means, but perhaps it was the highest.

'Lizzie?' Damon called out. 'I know you're in there. Please open the door.'

She took a few shaking breaths and then swung the door wide. No way did she want Damon thinking that she was hiding from him.

Resolutions were one thing, but seeing Damon again was another. At least he was prepared for the vagaries of the London weather, she registered, taking in his heavy jacket and tough, workmanlike boots. Damon would look hot in a monk's robes, and in a thick sweater and jeans he looked as darkly, wickedly stunning as usual—while *she* felt exhausted and hurt, and above all furiously angry.

Her body should recoil from him after what he'd done, but nothing had changed where that was concerned. Her heart still raced and her breathing still quickened at the sight of him. Worse. Her body yearned as if it had no sense—but this time there was anger in the mix.

'Yes?' she demanded crisply. 'What do you want?'

'*Theos,* Lizzie!' he exclaimed. 'Thank God you're home.' He raked his hair in a familiar gesture. 'Let me in. We need to talk—'

'More talking?' she said, still barring his way.

'We have to talk when our daughter's involved,' he insisted.

Damon was a picture of power and dominance standing on the damp London street, while *she* had prepared for nothing and was wearing a faded old top, pyjama bottoms, and a pair of furry slippers on her feet. Her face was scrubbed clean of make-up and her hair was scraped back. Not her armour of choice, but she'd take it.

'*Our* daughter?' she queried. 'Are you sure about that?'

Damon's frown deepened. 'Of course I'm sure. Can I come in now?'

She stood back, and tensed as he brushed past her. She'd forgotten how big he was. This entire London house would fit into the hallway of his beachside mansion. She hesitated before opening the door to her bedsit, hardly able to imagine that they'd both fit inside.

She didn't waste time on pleasantries—especially as Damon didn't look around with interest, as she might have expected, but focused solely on her face. Going to the table, she picked up the letter and fanned it in front of him.

Lifting her chin to stare him in the eyes, she demanded, 'Did you authorise this?'

Damon's expression blackened as he recognised

the name on the top of the letterhead. 'Of course not. What is it?'

'You don't know?'

'No, I don't,' he insisted. 'When did it arrive?'

'It was waiting for me when I got home.'

'May I?'

For the first time since she'd known him, she saw that Damon was badly thrown. She could hear it in his voice and see it in the deepness of the furrows between his eyes.

She handed him the letter and he read it quickly.

'Lizzie.' His eyes flicked up to meet her angry stare. 'I didn't ask for this.'

'So this firm of lawyers *doesn't* act for you?'

'You know it does. It must have been a terrible shock for you to recognise the name from your father's trial. I'm sure that's something you won't easily forgot.'

'Compassion? From you?' She huffed a laugh.

Could she believe him? Lizzie wondered. She wanted to, but sometimes it seemed that her whole life had been spent battling the disappointment of being let down.

'I felt sick to the stomach when I saw that letter.'

'This letter—this request for a DNA test,' he said, with what she was sure was genuine disgust, 'has *nothing* to do with me. Believe me, Lizzie. It's a matter of trust. You have to believe me.'

'I don't have to do anything.'

'You said you trusted me on the island,' Damon said steadily. 'Do you trust me now?'

She wanted to—so badly—but the past always stood in her way. 'I don't know what to think,' she confessed.

It didn't help that Damon's blistering glamour carried all the sultry heat of a Greek afternoon, which lent an aura of unreality to everything that was happening in the familiar surroundings of her small, cosy home. He could light up the damp London street without any help from the lamps outside, but could she trust him?

She really didn't know, Lizzie realised.

She felt as if she were being squeezed between Damon's lawyers, Damon's money, Damon, and an opulent lifestyle that was utterly alien to her. It was next to impossible to extract any judgement from that.

'I didn't send this,' he repeated softly, staring her in the eyes. 'I didn't ask for this letter to be drafted, let alone mailed to you. Your word is enough for me, Lizzie.'

Her word was enough for him? Trust was the most valuable currency of all in Lizzie's life, so why was she still holding back?

Because she had to make decisions for Thea too, Lizzie realised. This wasn't about her. It never had been. And she didn't know if she would ever feel confident enough to invite Damon in to their exclusive club of two.

'Will you be staying long?' she asked formally, feeling awkward, feeling edgy, feeling uncertain, when certainty was what she *had* to feel where everything to do with Thea was concerned.

'Apparently not,' Damon said dryly, putting the letter back on the table.

'I meant in London.'

'That depends,' he said.

She wouldn't give him the satisfaction of asking upon what it depended. She was in no mood to soften. This was her turf, her home, her sanctuary, and his lawyer's letter had breached that security.

'So, how did this happen?'

Damon shrugged. 'My legal team is over-keen.'

'That's not good enough.'

Not now the past had swooped over her like an ugly black cloak, blotting out the facts in front of her and replacing them with horrors from another day.

'What does it matter if you authorised this letter or not? Your legal team work for *you*, in your name, as they worked that day to destroy my father. Do I want to hang around to see if any more letters like this arrive? Do I want to subject Thea to the risk of finding one some day? If you love Thea, as you say you do, I suggest you take this letter and shove it up your lawyer's backside, where it belongs—'

But she couldn't wait for that, and so she shredded it instead and let the pieces drop through her fingers like a shower of toxic confetti.

He was tempted to applaud, but guessed that wouldn't go down well. Lizzie was never more magnificent than when she was defending their child. If he had the whole world to choose from he couldn't find a better woman than this. He only wondered that it had taken him so long to realise Lizzie's true worth. He guessed that while he was a speed freak in business, and had everything down to a well-oiled art where that was concerned, he was a little less adept when it came to handling emotions and human relationships.

'You don't get to tell me what to do here. This is *my* turf,' Lizzie was telling him.

He had the satisfaction of hearing the pieces of the lawyer's letter crunch beneath his boots as he moved towards her. He would have liked to grind them through the floorboards and consign them to hell.

'I quite agree,' he told her.

There was a silence, and then she said, 'You do?'

'Yes.' He shrugged. 'You're right. That letter should never have been sent, but *I'm* ultimately responsible for it. My legal team thought they were protecting me. I know,' he said as her eyes lit. 'I hardly need protecting. But you do. And Thea does too. And I should be first in line to do that.'

Lizzie eyes betrayed all the uncertainty inside her, while *he* was stripped down to his most vulnerable, with everything to lose.

He'd fought off emotion all his life, wanting to fight for, and protect his parents. He'd fight now, if he had to.

'I won't let Thea suffer because of my naiveté,' Lizzie said, obviously still tense and worried, 'so if there's a copy of that letter in a vault somewhere, or on a computer, I want it destroyed.'

'It will be,' he promised. 'Thea will never know about the letter unless you tell her.'

'Well, obviously I won't.'

'You're not to blame for any of this, Lizzie. You never were.'

Damon's will was vibrating in the room like a tangible thing, tempting her to believe him.

'So you don't think I'm a liar, like my father?'

'Of course I don't. Would I be here if I did?'

She'd needed to hear that, but she still had to shake her head to try and dislodge the memories. The faces of her father's victims were always with her, reminding her that she should be punished too. She had enjoyed her last birthday party at home before the trial, as the privileged daughter of a supposedly wealthy man. She had adored her dress and everything else about that night—without realising that she'd been drinking and eating and dancing at the expense of so many vulnerable victims.

If only she could have that time over again—time to make things right and stop her father. If only she'd known—

'Lizzie, you have to stop this,' Damon insisted quietly. 'I understand what you're going through, but you can't change the past, and nor can you go on blaming yourself for what your father did.'

Easy for him to say, but guilt was eating her alive. Did he know that?

'And I suppose I can't blame myself for my father's death?' she suggested. 'But I still do.'

'What are you talking about?'

'They offered me counselling before I went to visit him in jail for the first time. I knew within five minutes that the person counselling me had no idea. Beyond offering me a box of tissues, a few murmured platitudes, and telling me that it would be "good for me to talk", she had nothing to offer—while I still had to get my head around the basics, like finding somewhere to live and putting food on the table. I didn't have time to waste emoting. All I could think of was getting out of that office so I could get on with the rest of my life.'

'And did you?' Damon angled his chin to stare at her.

'Yes. That day in court changed me. My father's death changed me even more. It was a wake-up call and a turning point for me. It told me in stark language that it was time to grow up.'

'You did have a lot of changes to get used to.'

'You think?' She found a small wry smile. 'I had to get used to the world I believed in turning out to be a fantasy. Having my only living relative in prison and losing my friends didn't help…' Her voice tailed away.

'I don't see how that makes you responsible for your father's death,' Damon prompted.

'I was angry with him and I was homeless,' Lizzie remembered. 'By the time I had scraped together enough money for my first visit to the jail I got there and they said he was dead. He'd hanged himself.'

The feelings she'd suffered on that terrible day, swept over her now. They were weaker, of course. Time was kind like that. But the sense of abandonment had never truly left her. Like the grief at having any chance of making things right between Lizzie and her father stolen away, the shock of his death, and the realisation that time lost could never be recaptured, had changed her forever.

'*Theos*, Lizzie! You found out like that?'

'Exactly like that. It was kept out of the newspapers. The publicity wouldn't be good for the jail, they said. I'm over it now—of course I am,' she insisted. 'But after his death I went from feeling the weight of everyone's disapproval to suffering their pity—which was almost worse. A lot of people turned away, and I can't blame them. It was as if Dad and me had both been infected with the same disease. I just wish I could have done something more to help him. Hence the ongoing guilt, I suppose.'

'You were very young.'

'Old enough to have a child.'

'Your father chose your stepmother in preference to you,' Damon insisted. 'He wanted you in court because he thought you might be useful to him. That isn't love, Lizzie, that's taking advantage of someone's good nature—yours, in this instance.'

She felt naked and vulnerable, having bared her soul, and she went on the defensive immediately. 'You're very supportive, Damon. Will you give me the same level of support when I fight you for Thea?'

'I hope it doesn't come to that, but you can't keep our daughter from me.'

'You sound very sure.'

'I am. Because—'

'You have another team of lawyers?' Lizzie guessed.

'No,' Damon said carefully. 'I am sure it won't come to that. Because Thea has asked to see me.'

'Thea has— I'm sorry.' Lizzie paled. 'What did you say?'

'Thea has asked to see me now and again,' Damon explained. 'And that's what we've agreed on.'

'*You've* agreed this? Without consulting me?'

'Yes, Thea and I talked it over. We'll meet now and then…at least to begin with…and then, over time, we'll see more of each other, depending on how things go.'

'I can't get my head around this,' Lizzie said tensely. 'You've spoken to Thea without telling me?'

'She rang me. I could hardly refuse to speak to my own daughter.'

'Thea *rang* you?' Lizzie repeated foolishly. She felt as if the ground was shaking beneath her feet and every certainty she'd ever had was slipping away from her. 'You told me I could trust you…'

'You can,' Damon insisted.

'So you go behind my back and talk to my daughter—'

'*Our* daughter,' he interrupted. 'I gave Thea my number in case she ever needed it.'

'Why would she need it?' Lizzie challenged.

'I'm her father,' Damon said quietly. 'Who else would she call?'

'Me! She'd call *me*,' Lizzie insisted furiously. 'How could you do this? I'll never trust you again as long as I live. Get out. Get out now! *Get out!*'

She broke several nails flinging the door open.

In one breath Damon had denounced the letter and

accepted Thea as his daughter, and then in that self-same breath he had admitted that he was speaking to Thea behind Lizzie's back on a semi-regular basis.

To say she felt unnervingly threatened would be massively understating the case. She was on the outside looking in at a relationship that was obviously developing between Damon and Thea without her involvement. How had it come to this? Had Thea already made her choice as to where and with whom she wanted to live?

She had to tell herself not to be so ridiculous. Thea was an intelligent girl. They loved each other. Love like theirs couldn't be threatened or stolen away by anyone.

And when Damon strode out of the house without a backward glance, leaving Lizzie with no idea if she'd ever see him again, she wondered if maybe that was a *good* thing.

CHAPTER SIXTEEN

HE CALLED HER from the car. He had been sitting right around the corner from Lizzie's bedsit for almost an hour before he called. Her tiny room was not the right forum for big emotions to run wild.

He smiled faintly as he waited for her to pick up, imagining the answer he might get when she did. This passionate creature was the Lizzie he remembered, and while one part of him wanted nothing more than to reassure her that she had nothing to worry about another part of him was glad to have her back.

'Hello?' She sounded suspicious.

'Hey…'

'What do you want, Damon?' She sounded hostile.

'To fill in a few gaps for you.'

'You think that will help?' she demanded sceptically.

'It can't do any more harm.'

There was a long pause, and then she asked, 'Where are you?'

'Not far away.'

Silence.

'If it helps with all that guilt you're carrying around,' he said, deciding to be blunt, 'you should know that all your father's victims got their money back.'

'How could they?' she demanded. 'My father didn't have any funds left when he died. My stepmother saw to that.'

'The Gavros Foundation took care of it.'

'I should have known,' she murmured.

He waited.

'So I'm in your debt now?'

'You're in no one's debt,' he assured her. 'You were a victim as much as anyone else in that courtroom. I should have found a way to tell you what my family intended to do, but I was always too busy thinking about rebuilding the business.'

'That doesn't make me feel any less guilty,' she assured him. 'You shouldn't have *had* to rebuild your family business. You wouldn't have had to do that if my father hadn't defrauded yours.'

'Lizzie, if you're guilty I'm guilty too. I didn't spare a thought for the fallout of that day, beyond the financial implications for Gavros Inc. I seem to remember we'd had a good year, so it was no problem for the foundation to grant funds to the victims. Knowing they'd got their money back gave me a good feeling. But I didn't spare a thought for the emotional consequences. You're right. I was all about money then—ruthless and uncaring. I thought my duty was done, and that was enough.'

'And now?'

'And now I understand how incredibly courageous you've been.'

'Please,' she said wearily.

'I'm not patronising you. You were down on the floor and fate kept on kicking you. I only wish I'd been there to pick you up.'

'I didn't need anyone to pick me up,' she countered fast. 'I picked myself up. And about time too.'

'And now I need your agreement to move forward—the three of us together,' he explained.

'You didn't need my agreement to speak to Thea,' she pointed out with justifiable fire. 'So what's changed, Damon?'

'*I* have,' he admitted.

There was a long silence, and then she said, 'Where are you? And I want a GPS fix this time.'

He wondered if he'd ever felt so happy as he swung himself out of the car.

They met halfway down the street. Lizzie was in her slippers, with a coat thrown over her pyjamas.

'Can we start over?' Damon asked her as the rain started to pelt down.

'We'd better get back,' she said, pulling her coat over her head.

They ran for it, but by the time they got back to the house she was soaked.

And drained.

Exercising emotions was every bit as exhausting as a hard day's training at the gym, Lizzie had discovered, and after eleven years of holding things in that amounted to a *lot* of fatigue. The faintest of smiles on Damon's mouth was enough to bring her strength flooding back, but for how long? she wondered.

'You'd better come in,' she said. 'We'll talk in my room.'

'So you trust me now?' he said, leaning back against the door.

'Do I have an option?'

'No. And I've got a better idea than discussing this in your room. Come back to the island with me and we'll talk there. Not tonight. Sleep tonight, and tomorrow I'll come and get you.'

She was just figuring out the pros and cons of this when Damon seized the initiative. 'Where's your sense of adventure, Lizzie? All I've ever wanted is the best for you and Thea. And if you can't believe that believe this—'

Her world exploded into vivid colour as Damon drove his mouth down on hers. It was rain after a drought, a rock in a shifting sea of doubt and guilt. She wanted him—wanted this—tongues tangling and stroking in an arousing reminder of the act she longed for while she clung to him and he growled with pleasure as she pressed her body hungrily against his.

Eleven years of caution and protecting Thea with everything she'd got made it hard to give in to her own selfish pleasure, but with Damon's physical heat surrounding her, and her body begging her to relent, she was at least prepared to hear him out.

'What are you going to do?' she asked tensely when he released her.

'Heal you,' he said.

Damon left Lizzie in a tantalising state of extreme arousal after giving her instructions to pack. He'd seemed in a hurry to get somewhere, and she'd warned him that she wasn't very good at taking instructions. But she wasn't very good at feeling sorry for herself either. What good did it do?

When Damon's car had roared off and it was quiet again she felt lonely, standing on her own in the middle of an empty room in an empty house, and then she decided that she could sit down and cry or get on with things. She chose action.

First things first. She was hungry. An army fought on its stomach, and the Italian restaurant down the road was always bright and welcoming. She could walk there once she'd changed into some dry clothes. Right now pizza and a glass of rough red wine sounded like heaven.

Lizzie was carrying serious wounds from the past, and he couldn't be one hundred per cent sure of her unless he did something epic to reassure her that he really *had* turned a corner and was determined to see things through.

He was like a bear with a sore head as he drove away from her bedsit. The fact that his lawyer had acted without his authority still inflamed him. The man had been growing in confidence year on year, but this latest action had set Damon back eleven years. That legal firm was history—but that was the least of his worries now.

Needing space to think, he shifted lanes so he could take the long, straight road out of town. He got what he deserved—which was all the time in the world to work on his frustration as he battled with the sluggish evening traffic—but at least his mind cleared and he made a couple of calls. He had one possible ally, and he'd call in every card he'd got if it would make things right with Lizzie.

He'd told her to get some sleep?

Who the hell did he think he was?

Should she sleep? Sleep and dream? See all those faces in that courtroom again? He knew they haunted her. And he'd left her to deal with it on her own, so soon after the shock of receiving that lawyer's letter. To hell with that!

Swinging the wheel, he turned and headed back the way he'd come. Half an hour later he was finally getting somewhere—both in the car and with the project he had in mind. He was already calling Lizzie's number by the time he joined the traffic heading back into London.

'Where are you?' he demanded when she picked up.

'Where am I? Eating.' She sounded surprised to hear from him.

He could hear plates clattering in the background. 'Eating where?'

The silence continued until impatience was banging like cymbals in his head. 'Where *are* you, Lizzie?' he repeated tensely.

'In an Italian restaurant close to home—'

He cut the line and gunned the engine.

Some things were worth getting a speeding ticket for.

She'd been moving food around her plate for so long the waiters had started glancing anxiously at her. They had a reputation to uphold. The food at this restaurant was supposed to be the best in London outside of Italy. It certainly smelled good, but Lizzie hadn't managed more than a mouthful, and even that seemed to stick in her throat.

The wine helped, but she waved away the offer of another glass with a polite, 'No, thank you.'

What she *should* have done was tell Damon to come here, so they could talk things over before she did anything as rash as going back with him to Greece. It would have been easier here, surrounded by strangers in a busy restaurant.

'Penny for them...'

Breath shot out of her lungs. 'Damon?'

Framed in the doorway, Damon looked like a dark angel on a mission to seduce. Everyone in the busy restaurant obviously agreed with her, as every head had instinctively turned his way.

'May I join you?' he asked.

Who was going to stop him? She was as transfixed as every other sentient adult in the place. He looked vital and dangerous and a whole lot tastier than the pizza she'd been moving around her plate.

'Please.' She indicated the seat opposite hers in the secluded booth.

Within moments of him settling waiters were swarming.

'What are you doing with that pizza?' He stared with disapproval at her plate. 'Were you planning to re-sole your shoes with it, or maybe save it for a mid-night snack? We'll have two more of whatever this was,' he added, smiling at a waiter. 'It smells delicious. And a bottle of your best red, some olives, and a plate of antipasti to pick at…maybe some prosciutto and melon, grilled veggies, and a bowl of meatballs—'

'Damon!'

He put a restraining hand over hers. 'I'm a big man with a huge appetite, and I didn't realise how hungry I was until I walked through that door and smelled the food.'

Blood rushed to her cheeks. Damon was a game-changer. She should have remembered that. She tried not to blink or react at all when he nestled his legs comfortably against hers. Space was the problem. Space would always be the problem with Damon. And the booth was an intimate, secluded oasis—ideal for people who wanted a little privacy with their meal.

'Damon—no!' she said as his expression changed from genial, when the waiter was around, to something else as he studied her face.

'What do you mean, no?'

The tug at the corner of his mouth was the only warning Lizzie needed that things weren't going to go to plan. At least not to *her* plan.

'I'm not going to hear any more of these trust issues, am I?' he demanded. 'Because I've got something for you.' He settled back. 'And there's someone who wants to speak to you before I hand it over.'

Her heart started thumping as Damon brought out his phone.

He punched in a number on speed dial. 'Is that okay with you?' he asked, glancing at the phone in his hand as he waited for the call to connect.

'Depends on who it is,' Lizzie admitted.

Damon's expression brightened as the person he was calling answered the phone. 'Thea?'

Damon had *Thea* on speed dial? Lizzie blenched. Change she could cope with—but change this fast was something else again.

'What's going on?' she demanded, before taking the phone.

'Chill!' Thea exclaimed. 'I heard you. Don't be angry with Damon. I've got something to tell you.'

'Obviously…' Lizzie tried to sound bright, and only succeeded in sounding tense and concerned.

'Don't sound so worried,' Thea said, reading Lizzie with her usual ease.

'I'm not worried,' Lizzie said, still tense.

'You're going to like this—I promise,' Thea said confidently.

Right now, Lizzie doubted it. 'Just tell me what it is,' she prompted, forcing a smile into her voice.

'Surprises are always the best, aren't they?' Thea enthused, giggling and obviously surrounded by her friends.

'I *do* love surprises,' Lizzie agreed, trying not to sound as if surprise right at this moment equated with a visit to the dentist.

'But that all depends what the surprise *is*, doesn't it, Mama?'

'Do you always have to be so smart?'

As Thea broke into peals of laughter Lizzie shot a keen look at Damon, trying to read his face.

'Damon's got it,' Thea announced, almost choking on her giggles. 'Let him show you the surprise. He wanted to get you something to say sorry, and I told him what you'd like. You *will* give him a chance to say sorry, won't you? Like in the last scene of all the best movies?'

'What have you done?' Lizzie mouthed, staring at Damon, who merely shrugged.

'Sorry—I have to go now!' Thea yelled. 'We're having movie night at school.'

Hence the reference, Lizzie thought as she clutched the phone, wishing she could give Thea a hug instead.

'Won't be long until school breaks up for summer—and then we're off to Greece again,' Thea announced with excitement. 'Night-night!' she exclaimed, before Lizzie could ask any more questions.

And with that the line was cut and Thea was gone.

Thea and Damon were not only in contact with each other, they were arranging holidays together now...

'You should have told me,' she said quietly. 'You *have* to keep me in the loop, Damon.'

He huffed agreement. 'I guess I'll get there eventually.'

'Damn right you will,' Lizzie said, getting up to leave the booth.

Damon grabbed her wrist, stopping her. 'Our food's on its way—'

'So?' She stared angrily at his hand on her arm until he removed it.

'Sit down,' he murmured, almost winning her over with a smile. 'I want to give you the gift I told you about.'

'It will have to wait,' she said coolly. 'I need time to—'

'To do *what*, Lizzie? You've had all the time in the world, as far as I can tell.'

She ground her jaw and then sat down again. 'This had better be good.'

'I hope you think so,' Damon agreed as he delved into the pocket of his jacket.

When he pulled out a battered ring case she was speechless.

'I want you to have this—whatever you decide to do next.' He pushed the black velvet box across the table towards her.

She hardly dared touch it.

'Thea would never forgive me if I didn't sort this out for you,' Damon explained. 'I felt so bad about the incident with the violin that I asked Thea how I could make up for it, and she said with this. She said she'd promised to get it back for you one day, and that this was her chance to make good on her word. It was the first time she called me Dad,' he added softly.

Lizzie closed her hand around the ring case. There was so much to take in.

'To be exact,' Damon added wryly, changing the mood and brightening it, 'Thea told me to, "Go get it, Dad. And remember this is just your *first* test."'

'That *does* sound like Thea,' Lizzie admitted as she caressed the ring case with her fingertips.

'Aren't you going to open it?'

'I'm not sure I dare.'

'I'm sure you do dare,' Damon argued softly. 'There's nothing you don't dare, from what I remember. If there's one thing I've learned about you, Lizzie, it's that you've got more guts than most people. So open the box and wear the ring. Think of your mother when you wear it. Think how happy she'd be to know that you've got it back. And remember this isn't a gift from me to you—this is a gift to you from Thea. Let the ring be the symbol of our new start…all three of us. It will make Thea happy to see you wearing it, and I think it completes the circle. Don't you agree?'

I'll heal you, he'd said, Lizzie remembered as Damon opened the ring case and took out her mother's ring.

She thanked him when he slipped the simple band onto her finger. 'Thank you' seemed inadequate for something like this, but she said it anyway.

'Don't thank me—thank Thea,' he said as she stared down at the distinctive ring with its three tiny seed pearls set snugly in the golden band.

'Thank you,' Lizzie repeated softly, lifting her gaze to meet Damon's.

'You don't have to thank a man who loves you for anything,' he insisted, smiling into her eyes.

The short time that remained before school was out for summer was spent packing up the bedsit and putting everything Lizzie cared about into storage. The rest went to the thrift shops that Thea loved so much— though Thea did keep back a few battered articles.

'We're not necessarily staying on the island for good,' Lizzie had warned.

She and Damon had started over. They hadn't slept together or even kissed since the night of the ring and Damon telling her that he loved her. The tension between them was ferocious, but it was all part of making that fresh start, he'd said.

Lizzie had thought she knew how she wanted things to go, which was slowly, but the more she saw of Damon the more she wanted to let the past go— to learn from it, certainly, but never to let it rule her again.

Damon's private jet took Lizzie and Thea to the island, where he was waiting for them on the Tarmac. Thea had no inhibitions and flung herself into her father's arms. Thea had always embraced life wholeheartedly, Lizzie thought, glad that she could. Life required a healthy dose of courage, and self-belief never went amiss. Thea would need those qualities if she was to give confidence to others in her turn.

'The ring worked like the magic charm I said it would!' Thea exclaimed to Damon, with a happy glance at Lizzie.

Resting his sunglasses on top of his head, Damon smiled into Lizzie's eyes. 'So you're still wearing it?'

'Always,' Lizzie whispered.

Putting his arm around both of them, Damon escorted them to his SUV and saw them safely settled inside. The drive to the beach house was tense—but for all the right reasons, Lizzie thought as she sat up front with Damon. She tried not to look at him, not to register him at all, conscious that their daughter was sitting behind them and noticing everything. But she was entirely, acutely, lovingly aware of him.

There were more surprises to come. Damon didn't take them to the beach house, but to his old family home.

'I swopped houses with my parents,' he explained. 'My mother has always lusted after the beach house, so I asked Thea which house *you'd* prefer and she said this one.'

Lizzie was speechless—and not the slightest bit put out that Damon had sprung the surprise, because this *was* her true dream home.

'There's still a studio where you can paint, and a music room for Thea, but you can change things around any way you want,' Damon explained. 'No pressure for either of you. You can come here whenever you like, or don't come at all. The house is in your name, Lizzie. I signed it over to you. Lawyers can be useful sometimes,' he added with a wry smile.

'It's mine?' Lizzie exclaimed. 'But you can't—'

'I can and I have,' Damon assured her. 'I know a house can't make up for all the years you spent on your own, but I hope it goes some way to saying that I love you both, and that I want you both in my life. And you, Lizzie, will have something of your own now—something to sell or to keep or to do whatever you want. All expenses are fully covered, of course—'

'No.'

'Mama!'

'I can't accept that.'

'Why not?' Thea demanded.

'Are you two in league?' Lizzie found it hard to be angry with Thea, who had never once complained when they were short of money.

'If you mean, do we want to work together for your happiness, Thea and me, then the answer to that has to be yes,' Damon assured her. 'And there's one more thing I have to ask you.'

'Ask away. You might as well get it all off your chest,' Lizzie conceded.

She was stunned when Damon dropped to one knee at her feet.

'I never thought I'd feel the need to do this,' he said, 'but I do. I *so* do. Will you marry me, Lizzie? Will you spend the rest of your life with me?'

Damon had taken hold of her hand, and now he took hold of Thea's hand.

'Can we be a family at last—a *happy* family?' he added for Thea's benefit. 'We've still got a lot of work to do,' he admitted with his usual bluntness, 'but when we work to the power of three I don't know who's going to stop us, do you?'

It took her a moment to take everything in, but then Lizzie went to her knees in front of Damon. 'I certainly won't stand in your way,' she teased him softly.

He laughed.

And when Thea knelt to join them Lizzie said, 'For all of us, my answer to your question is absolutely *yes*.'

He'd waited to make Lizzie his bride for long enough, Damon informed Lizzie the next morning, so they would get married on the island that same week by special licence—with Thea as their bridesmaid and Iannis and Stavros as their witnesses.

'I hope you don't mind that I've already made plans,' Damon said as the two of them lay entwined in bed.

'There are some plans I'm quite happy for you to make without any direction from me,' Lizzie teased him lightly. 'Though I did think you meant that you couldn't wait for our wedding night.'

'That too,' he said, brushing her hair aside to kiss the angry tiger cub. 'And also this—'

'What?' she said as he leaned over the side of the bed.

Opening a drawer in the nightstand, Damon brought out a small jeweller's box. 'Wedding and engagement ring all in one,' he explained. 'I hope you're all right with that?'

When Lizzie opened the box she was speechless. The band was exquisite. Chased gold, with a flawless emerald cut diamond set in the centre of it, the ring was spectacular. It was everything she would have chosen for herself, way back when fairytales had been her usual night-time reading, but it was the inscription inside the ring that really choked her up.

For the love of my life.

And there was a date. Damon had charted their love from the first night they'd met.

'Full circle,' he said.

'For ever,' Lizzie agreed.

Drawing her into his arms, Damon removed the ring box from her fingers and placed the symbol of their love on her hand.

EPILOGUE

ALL OF LIZZIE'S dreams came true under a cobalt blue sky on a sugar sand beach, barefoot in the arms of the man she loved.

Stavros and Iannis had got together with their wives to ensure there was a flower-strewn canopy where their wedding ceremony would be held, and guests came from all over the island to see Lizzie in a simple gown that slipped over her head and clung to her body like a delicately embroidered, diaphanous second skin.

She was sure the flimsy ankle-length gown must have cost Damon a fortune, though he'd completely blown her mind by supplying her with an entire rail of dresses to choose from.

'No reason why my bride should suffer because I can't wait to marry her,' he'd said.

'Don't look so worried. I found half of them in a thrift shop,' Thea had added, with a mischievous glance at her father.

'Yeah,' Lizzie had agreed wryly, 'a thrift shop named—'

'Does it matter where they came from?' Damon had interrupted. 'They've been bought with love. Accept them.'

Now she'd sold her first painting she might just do that, Lizzie thought. Who would have known that her happiness-infused watercolours of the island would sell so well?

The Internet made everything immediate, and she might only have been back on the island for a short while, but her head was buzzing with ideas for paintings and it seemed to Lizzie that she'd found a fresh calling—better than washing dishes, though the only downside was that her nails were now customarily rimmed with paint.

As everyone cheered the newly married couple Thea joined in with the local band on an improvised stage to salute them with a resoundingly popular solo.

'Maybe I *will* be a violinist, after all,' she told Damon and Lizzie, before racing off to join the friends she would be staying with during her parents' honeymoon.

Whatever their daughter wanted to be was all right with them, Lizzie thought as she shared a glance with Damon. They both wanted the same thing for Thea, and that was for their daughter to do what she wanted to do and be happy doing it.

'I guess I'll have to work harder at this family thing than I ever had to work at business,' Damon admitted as he brought Lizzie into his arms.

'You better had—'

'I will,' he promised softly, in a way that made her body yearn. 'Starting now…'

'*What*—where are you taking me?' Lizzie demanded as Damon carried her through the line of cheering guests. 'What about our wedding reception?'

'Our wedding has been unconventional, and the same goes for our wedding reception,' Damon informed her. 'The feasting will continue without us. We'll be back in a week's time for a celebratory party with our friends—'

'And where are we going in the meantime?' Lizzie asked.

'Some call it paradise,' Damon told her solemnly as he strode towards the waiting helicopter. 'I just call it bed.'

'I'm good with that,' Lizzie agreed.

'*Agapi mou*, you're the love of my life,' Damon assured her with a soft, husky laugh. 'And I need at least a week to prove that to you before the rest of our happily married life can continue—or I will surely die of frustration.'

'Me too,' Lizzie said, nestling close in the arms of the man she adored.

* * * * *

If you enjoyed
THE SECRET KEPT FROM THE GREEK,
why not try these other
SECRETS HEIRS OF BILLIONAIRES
themed stories?

DEMETRIOU DEMANDS HIS CHILD
by Kate Hewitt
THE DESERT KING'S SECRET HEIR
by Annie West
THE SHEIKH'S SECRET SON
by Maggie Cox
THE INNOCENT'S SHAMEFUL SECRET
by Sara Craven
THE GREEK'S PLEASURABLE REVENGE
by Andie Brock

Available now!